FALLING FOR BEN & OTHER IMPOSSIBLE THINGS

THE GARCIA BROTHERS, BOOK 1

YESENIA VARGAS

I'm gonna pull a Snoop Dogg here and say…
I want to thank me, for everything I've done for me.

And as always, to all of my readers…
THANK YOU.

1

JEFFERSON HIGH CAME into focus through the passenger window.

I exhaled a long breath as Mom pulled into the morning car rider line.

First day at a new school.

Maybe here we'd get that new start Mom and I so desperately needed.

Students buzzed around the busy parking lot and the tidy green campus.

It was a lot nicer than my old school.

I stared out the window, a little nervous, my backpack in my lap.

Mom followed the morning car rider line at a snail's pace until we were at the curb at the front of the school.

I turned to her.

She gave me a tight-lipped smile. "This is it," she said. Her dark hair fell in long waves around her shoulders. Between her hair, make up, and navy blue blazer, she looked like a total boss. "Make some friends, okay? And have a really good day."

I nodded, doing my best to smile back. "Thanks, Mom. I'll try." I paused, glancing at her. "Although you never seem to have problem with that. Making friends, I mean."

Unlike me.

She finally gave me a real smile, the kind that made her eyes scrunch up a little bit and gave her those crow's lines she hated so much. "What can I say? People can't help but see that I'm amazing."

I laughed, not realizing how much I needed it. "If you could give me just a little bit of that, it would be awesome."

She pinched my cheek. "You're gonna be fine. Just smile. And don't be afraid to say hi first instead of staring at people like this."

Mom did a ridiculous deer in headlights look.

I laughed some more. "That may or may not be an accurate representation of me in social situations."

The car rider line moved up a little bit more, and I put my hand on the door. "I should go. Kill it at your new job, okay?"

She put both hands back on the steering wheel and grinned. It was easy to see how excited she was. "I will, hon. Text me and let me know how it goes, okay? I'll be home for dinner."

I nodded. "Okay." I stepped outside, the cool morning air hitting my face.

"You have your key, right?" she called, already moving forward slowly to keep up with the moving line.

"Yeah," I said, waving.

"Okay, sweetie!" she yelled way too loudly. "Have a good first day!"

A couple of cars honked at her, but that didn't faze Mom. With one last victorious smile and big wink, she drove off, leaving me to contemplate my social reputation at Jefferson—or what was left of it.

I stood there a second, refusing to look around and see just who had witnessed my mom saying goodbye loud enough to scare the birds away from the trees. Half the school had to have heard it.

Some kid in a black t-shirt and Vans walked by and actually snorted into his Starbucks from trying not to laugh.

With a shake of my head, I spun around and went inside. As embarrassing as that was, I could never be mad at Mom. She usually made it her goal to make me laugh and bring a smile to my face. Sometimes she took it a little overboard, but it sure beat dwelling on the past.

So her antics meant a lot.

I made my way to the front office and gave the lady a nervous smile. "Hi, I'm new. I need to pick up my schedule."

"Welcome to Jefferson High!" she replied.

Was it me or was she as loud and as enthusiastic as my mom?

"You're going to love it here," she went on. The name plate on her desk read KATHY WEISMAN. "What's your name, dear, and I'll print your schedule off so you can be on your way."

Oh. Duh. "Scarlett Moore. Two Ts."

"What a beautiful name," she said, her bright red fingernails clicking away at her keyboard.

I shifted my weight and hung onto the straps of my backpack, wondering what time first period started. "Thanks." I did not want to be late to my first class.

She went on, kind of muttering under her breath as she focused on the screen in front of her. "Ah, yes. Your transcripts came through and everything."

The sound of the printer made me sigh in relief. She grabbed the piece of paper it had just spit out and handed it to me. "Here you go. Your first class is Human Anatomy & Physiology with Mrs. Collins in room 542. That's just one building over. Quickest way is that way." She pointed to a wide hallway outside the office.

I nodded. "Thank you."

She gave me one last smile. "Of course. Cafeteria's on the way there if you need to grab breakfast." The phone rang loudly as she finished speaking.

She picked up. I left the front office and made my way down the hallway, maneuvering past groups of people talking and laughing and couples with their arms around each other.

One teacher, an older lady with bright blue spectacles, called out to a guy and girl kissing behind a locker door. "Mr. Sanchez, Ms. Kelly, separate!"

I grinned and kept going. Some things were the same no matter what school you ended up at.

Three girls chatted animatedly on the opposite side of the hallway. One of them donned a high ponytail of thick, shiny, black hair along with a wide grin. She said something that made her friends laugh.

She reminded me of Anne, one of my friends from my old school. She was in Massachusetts, over a hundred miles away, starting first period without me.

My heart twanged at the thought of not knowing anybody here. At the fact that I'd never lived anywhere besides my hometown, and now it was no longer home.

Did I even have a home? This sure didn't feel like home yet.

Our house had moving boxes everywhere, and I kept forgetting where everything in the kitchen was or how to leave the neighborhood.

And this school was full of strangers.

How would I ever be happy here? Would I ever belong here?

Even though I was surrounded by people, I hadn't felt more alone in a long time.

I reached the end of the hallway and entered a catwalk connecting this building to the next.

Before opening the double doors, I paused, part of me wishing I could just stay out there instead of having to do this.

My gaze went to a small garden in between the buildings. There was a bench in the middle of it that called to me.

But I wasn't the type to skip class. It just wasn't in my blood.

Anne, though, she would've rolled her eyes and told me if anyone deserved to take a little break it was me.

I turned back around and went through the double doors, pulling out my schedule as I walked. Room 542.

A bell rang, and I noticed that hardly anyone was left roaming the hallways. Scanning the classrooms I passed, I wondered if I was getting any closer.

Room 439. 437. 435.

Where was 542?

There had been a smaller hallway off to the side when I had come in. Maybe it was that way.

I spun around quickly, horrified at the thought of not finding Room 542, especially before the final bell rang.

Just like that, my head hit something both soft and solid.

I stumbled back, catching myself before landing on my butt.

What had just happened?

My eyes found a gray Jefferson hoodie and slowly slid up to the face of the guy wearing it.

Whoa.

I'd never seen eyes more green than the ones staring down at me.

My mouth hung open slightly, and I struggled to find words, any words, to indicate that I was in fact human and not some sort of malfunctioning robot. "Uh, sorry, I…didn't—"

"My fault," Green Eyes said, taking a couple of steps back. "Are you okay?"

I blinked a few times, my brain taking its sweet time processing his words, too busy memorizing the cadence of his voice.

It was just the right amount of deep, and his shoulders? Just the right amount of wide and strong.

His brow furrowed as he studied me. "You didn't bump your head too hard, did you?" he asked, now sounding a little worried.

That got me right out of my stupor. "No…no. I'm okay. Just caught by surprise, I guess."

I saw the schedule in my hand and remembered the reason I had even spun around so quickly and almost gotten run over by him. "Um, actually, do you know where room 542 is? I'm new and…"

Lost, I wanted to say. Luckily, though, he came a little closer and took a look at my schedule instead of waiting for me to finish a complete sentence.

Which seemed impossible with him this close.

I caught the scent of his cologne and almost missed his response.

What was wrong with me?

"Yeah, Mrs. Collins. I have her fourth period. Her classroom is upstairs," he said. Then he pointed back toward the double doors, to a door on the left. "The stairwell is right there. Her room isn't far."

I went over that again in my head, making sure I had heard him correctly and still staring toward the stairwell.

Then I turned back around. "Thank—" But he was already gone, the sound of his sneakers echoing in the hallway as he rounded the corner.

"You," I finished, alone.

By the time I made it up the stairs and found Mrs. Collins's room, the bell had rung.

Thankfully, she saw me coming down the hallway and held the door open for me.

She had kind brown eyes and curly blonde hair. "Welcome. You must be my new pupil."

"Scarlett Moore," I replied. "Nice to meet you."

"Happy to have you, Scarlett. There's an empty seat right over there," she said, closing the door and making her way to the board.

Front row. Great.

The chatting died down with the sound of the door banging shut and the sight of me at the front of the room.

I sat down quickly and got out a blank notebook and pencil.

Introducing myself to the whole class was the last thing I wanted to do. Thankfully, Mrs. Collins started the lesson right away, sparing me the humiliation.

Thank goodness for kind teachers.

She certainly seemed cool. Most of the class participated, and she had jokes. Funny ones. The girl next to me smiled and gave a little wave. Long strawberry blonde hair fell past her shoulders.

I grinned back and exhaled. First period was off to a good start. That had to be a sign.

Maybe moving to this town would end up being way better than I could've expected. All I knew was that I wanted to give it a fair shot.

While I took notes on the nervous system, though, I couldn't help but think of the guy from downstairs, the one with the vibrant jade eyes.

Another thing you could count on, no matter what high school in America you ended up in?

The extremely handsome boy you couldn't help but turn into a puddle of goo in front of.

I had no idea what his name was, but he had made my breath stop and heart pound all the same.

The more I thought about it, the more I decided how dorky I must have come across.

I shut my eyes, wishing I could do it over. Play it cool. Toss my hair over my shoulder and smile wide.

Exude a little self-confidence.

But no.

Instead, I had barely made a coherent sentence the entire time.

I could've cried from realizing what a weirdo he must've thought I was.

No wonder he'd run off to class.

I bit the inside of my lip.

What else could I have expected from my first day at Jefferson?

Hopefully in a school this big, I wouldn't have to worry about running into him again.

Even if part of me definitely wanted to.

2

IT WASN'T long before I saw him again.

Green eyes and me? We had the same lunch period.

Of course we did.

Part of me was thrilled. Obsessing a little over the cute jock was way better than first day jitters and figuring out where I was going to sit.

And a jock he was.

That part was obvious. His hoodie, rolled up to the elbows, had a panther and a football on it. A couple of his buddies wore school gear too, and it was obvious from their build that they were athletes. The way they sat on those tables, with their wide grins? They may as well have worn labels saying HOT & POPULAR STUDENT ATHLETE.

Not to mention the cheerleader-type girls around them.

Yep, those guys were definitely on the football team.

I tried not to stare while I grabbed napkins and plasticware.

Nora, a girl from my third period, walked up next to me, pulling napkins from the dispenser. "His name is Ben Garcia, and you wouldn't be first girl to stare at him like that."

She winked and smiled.

I blushed. "That obvious, huh?"

She laughed a little. "I don't blame you. Not one bit." She glanced toward one of the tables and then at me. "Want to sit with us?"

I could've hugged her. "I'd love to."

Mom was right. All I had to do was smile and I'd make friends. Although in my case, it had been smiling toward the hot guy and then getting caught.

Nora and I sat down a few tables away from the jocks.

The same girl with the friendly smile in first period was there. It turned out her name was Audrey.

We ate lunch, and Nora and Audrey told me some stuff about Jefferson.

Audrey dipped her French fry in ranch. "Mrs. Collins coaches the cheer squad, which is kind of a big deal around here."

Nora nodded toward the football players. "Along with the varsity football team. They usually go to State every year. It's all the principal cares about. He used to play here once upon a time too."

Audrey giggled. "Although you couldn't tell now."

A few minutes later, one of Audrey's friends joined us. I recognized the jet black hair and gleaming smile. It was the girl from this morning.

She held out her hand. "I'm Rachel. What's your name?"

I shook it. "Scarlett. I'm new."

She smiled. "Welcome to Jefferson, Scarlett," she replied. She picked up her fork and dug in. Then we all went back to talking. Or rather me listening to them talk about everything they had going on.

I laughed at a witty comment from Rachel but eyed Ben again. Unlike most of the other guys, I noticed that he didn't really talk much. He said hi to some of the girls, but he didn't ogle them or flirt with them like everyone else.

It was interesting.

Audrey gave Rachel this knowing look then turned back to me. Nora covered her mouth with her hand.

I looked down, a little embarrassed. They had to think I was so weird. "Sorry."

Rachel smiled. "Hey, when it comes to the Garcia brothers, we get it. They are…beyond cute."

"Brothers?" I asked. There were more of them?

Rachel nodded. "Yep. Plural. Their little brother is still in junior high, but Ben over there is the oldest."

"Arguably the cutest," Nora added. "Some days it's debatable," she added with a wink.

I giggled, wondering when I would get to see the other brothers.

Rachel leaned forward. "Unfortunately, Ben is the one brother who doesn't date. He doesn't do girlfriends or even ask girls to prom. Nothing."

With a quick glance back at him, I shook my head a little. "Why?"

Why would the cutest guy in the entire school say no to dating?

I mean, I'd only been a student at Jefferson High for a few hours. No way had I seen the entire boy population in that amount of time, but one thing I knew for sure. Ben was THE guy at Jefferson.

Tall, tan, athletic, and handsome.

Rachel shrugged and turned to Audrey and Nora.

Audrey kept her voice low but casual. "I hang out with Cade a lot, and he says football is too important to him. Not to mention he has like two jobs to help his mom cover bills and stuff."

Ben gave a yawn, covering his mouth. All of a sudden, I could see faint circles under his eyes. His hair was messy, and I thought before that it was on purpose, but now I realized maybe he just hadn't had time to pull a comb through it.

Don't get me wrong. The bedhead look worked on him.

But what Audrey was saying made sense.

"That's too bad," I heard myself say. Then I turned back to my food.

Rachel shrugged again. "It is what it is. Believe me, you're not the first girl to be sorely disappointed by Ben Garcia not doing the dating thing."

"You too?" I teased.

The hint of a smile played at Nora's face. "Not quite."

Rachel threw a French fry at her.

I looked between them. "What?"

Audrey grinned as Rachel took a swig of her water. "She has it bad for one of the other brothers."

Rachel coughed a little, and the rest of us laughed. "Okay, change of subject!" she said. "So, Scarlett. What's your thing?"

"My thing?" I replied. "What do you mean?"

Audrey and Nora waited for a response.

Rachel nodded. "Yeah. Your thing. Mine is cheer. Audrey's into music and stuff. Nora…well, Nora is just kinda weird, but we love her."

"Hey!" Nora laughed and pushed her playfully.

"What about you?" Rachel finished. "What are you into?"

I thought about that for a second. One thing came to mind. "Well, I was on the dance team back at my old school."

The girls looked thoroughly impressed.

"Dance?" Rachel said. "Like, did you compete and stuff?"

I nodded and kept eating. "Sometimes we did pretty well." I had a few medals to show for it.

Audrey turned to me. "Makes sense. You totally have a dancer's body."

"Thanks," I said with a smile. "I love it. My mom is a good dancer. I must have inherited it from her."

It was kind of our thing. We loved dancing, whether it was hip hop or merengue. Mom was half Latina so it was in our blood.

If I could get on the dance team here, then it would be awesome. I definitely missed it. "Does Jefferson have a dance team?" I asked.

Audrey shook her head. "No. Sorry."

Nora gave me an empathetic look. "The closest you're gonna get is cheer, and I have to say I'd recommend band over cheer."

She sounded serious until a teasing smile gave it away.

"Hey!" Rachel cried. "Our cheer squad is awesome, thank you very much. That's a biased yet true opinion," she huffed. Then she looked at me. "Seriously, though, Scarlett, our squad does a lot of dancing, not just cheering, in our routines. Our tryouts are tomorrow afternoon. You should totally come."

"Tomorrow afternoon?" I asked, hesitation clear in my voice. That was kind of soon. "I don't know. Maybe I'll take a break this semester. You know, get settled and make sure my grades are up."

Rachel rolled her eyes. "Grades? Really?"

Nora snorted a little, and Audrey cracked a smile.

Rachel went on. "I mean, yeah, grades are important, blah, blah, blah, but you're new here. If you want to fit in, not to mention make tons of friends and have fun every Friday night with CUTE FOOTBALL PLAYERS then I highly recommend joining the cheer squad." She grinned triumphantly, like no person in their right mind would say no to that.

But I had my doubts. I had been at Jefferson for one day, and she wanted me to commit to cheer? "I don't know, Rachel. I mean, I've never done cheer before. I don't think I'd be very good."

Plus the thought of me in that tiny skirt and top? I

mean, Mom would love it and take about a million pictures, but me? I wasn't so sure about this.

"Oh, come on!" Rachel said. "Promise me you'll at least think about it. We could use someone like you."

I opened my mouth to argue, but she kept going. "You said you guys did pretty well sometimes!"

"I'm just not sure I'm the cheerleader…type," I said, not quite meeting her eyes and doing my best not to sound like a jerk.

Nora began laughing, and Audrey held back a smile.

Rachel put her hands on her hips. "I don't know what the cheer squad back at your old school was like, Scarlett, but I promise we're not all airheads here. The girls are actually pretty cool. We hang out all the time, and like I said, Friday nights are even more fun down on the field instead of in the stands."

I glanced at Ben.

No, he would not be the reason I said yes or no to this.

I met Rachel's eyes. "I'll…think about it."

3

RACHEL FOUND me first thing the next morning. "Where's your gym bag? You said you'd think about it!"

I gave her my best "please don't hate me" smile. "I don't think I'm going to try out." Her face immediately fell, and I tried to explain. "I don't have anything ready, and I'm probably not gonna make it anyway. I promise I wouldn't know what I'm doing."

Rachel practically deflated but gave me a half smile at least. "It's okay. I get it."

Then she walked me to my next class, her arm in mine.

I had to hand it to her.

Rachel came on a little strong, but she was kind. Audrey and Nora too. I couldn't believe it was only my second day at Jefferson, and somehow, I'd already made some friends. It helped that Audrey and Nora had been nice to me from the start.

I waved goodbye to Rachel and went into class. A little bit of guilt made its way into my stomach. Rachel had been so cool about me turning her down. The least I could've done was go to tryouts, even if I didn't make it.

So what if I made a fool of myself in front of everyone? What were friends for? She'd definitely been a friend in the past day, lending me her notes in math and making sure I knew where I was going.

Then again, I just wasn't sure about potentially becoming a cheerleader.

What if I did make the squad?

That possibility was even worse than falling on my face in front of the prettiest, most confident girls at Jefferson.

This was a new school, where no one really knew me yet.

Did I want my identity to be that of cheerleader?

That was the last thing I'd ever seen myself as, and I wasn't sure I wanted to start now.

At the end of the day, I put away my books in my locker, only grabbing what I needed for homework that night.

The gym wasn't far, so I could hear the sound of basketballs bouncing around. A group of girls in sky-high ponytails and carrying bright gym bags walked past me and into the gym.

Including Rachel. She gave me a kind smile and quick wave before joining the rest of the squad inside the gym.

Now it was my turn to sigh.

I looked down at my blue jeans and over-sized

sweater. Then I pulled on my backpack and headed into the gym.

I was sooo going to regret this, but whatever.

After going into the girls' locker room, I found Rachel and gave her a nervous wave in the form of a large rainbow.

She looked at me, clearly confused as she eyed my outfit. "Scarlett, is everything okay? What are you doing here?"

I shrugged. "I'm trying out."

She laughed but not in a mean way, more like disbelief. "You said you weren't going to. Listen, it's okay if cheer isn't your thing."

I thought about that for a second. "I know. I just feel like it's the least I could do, you know? Do this for you and see if maybe cheer could be my thing. It's not the same as dance, but—"

I did miss dance…Cheer wasn't the same, but maybe it would be something?

Rachel wrapped me in a tight hug, then took a quick step back. "Tell me you're wearing something under that tent of a sweater."

I laughed a little. "Thanks. And yes, I am." Still not ideal cheer tryout clothing, but it would do.

After joining the rest of the girls in the gym, I took off my sweater, leaving it on the bleachers. Good thing I had worn high-waisted jeans that day.

The shirt I was wearing stopped just above my belly button. I hadn't planned on taking off my sweater today. This wasn't the kind of thing I usually wore to school.

Rachel walked over to me, eyeing my figure. "Girl, is it hot in here or is it just you? Don't let Ben see you."

I shook my head but grinned. "As if."

The loud and shrill sound of a whistle practically made me jump. Mrs. Collins stepped onto the court, the silver whistle still in her mouth. She let it drop to her chest and put her hands on her hips. "Ladies! Let's get warmed up."

Her eyes found mine while I stretched. "Scarlett." She paused. "I didn't expect to see you here, but I'm pleasantly surprised."

I smiled back. "Thanks. I wasn't planning on trying out," I said, indicating my clothes," but Rachel convinced me at the last minute."

Mrs. Collins nodded. "I wouldn't usually let you try out without the proper attire, but you're new, so I'll make an exception. I can't wait to see what you can do."

She gave me a wink and continued walking, reminding everyone to stretch their hamstrings or demonstrating the correct way to stretch.

I took a deep breath, now a little nervous because I had no idea what to expect. Eyeing my sweater on the bleachers across the gym, a big part of me wished I was on my way home to a couple hours of Netflix instead of preparing to make a fool of myself at cheerleading tryouts.

CHEERLEADING TRYOUTS.

I could hardly believe I was there.

What had I been thinking?

At my old school, the cheerleaders had been the last

girls I would ever choose to interact with. They may as well have been pulled from Mean Girls.

I blew out a breath and tried to focus on the instructions Mrs. Collins was giving us.

Something about earning points for this and deducting points for that. "And remember to smile! Very important."

Smile. Got it.

Didn't get much of anything else.

I tried not to throw up.

Pretended this was just like dance, except there wouldn't always be music.

It would be over before I knew it. Hopefully with minimal embarrassment.

A tall slender girl with dark hair like mine stepped up to the front next. "As you all know," she began. Then her gaze found mine. "Or most of you know. I'm Lily, this year's captain. I'll be demonstrating the moves that you'll be scored on. Do your best to do what I do with precise form and enthusiasm. We're not looking for perfection, so don't worry if you don't get all of the steps of the routine exactly right. We're more interested in your attitude and how you handle pressure. You guys ready?"

Just about everyone nodded, and I took a deep breath.

Not really, but what choice did I have?

(Insert a dozen nervous laughter emojis here.)

Lily gave us a big grin. "Good. Let's do this."

She pulled over a chair with a bluetooth speaker and took out her phone. A few taps later, she stood back up and handed it to Mrs. Collins, who stood at the ready with clipboard in hand. The rest of us moved well out of her way.

Lily took a soldier-like stance, much like we did on the dance team before the start of the routine. Straight arms at her side, big smile, thousand-mile stare.

Mrs. Collins hit play and the music came on.

A few seconds into the hip hop song, Lily began by putting her hands in the air, a pop of the hips to the left, pop of the hips to the right while she crossed her arms. Step forward, one-eighty. I bobbed my head slightly as I counted the beats in my head and visualized myself doing the same moves Lily was doing.

Lily came to a stop, and Mrs. Collins hit pause. Lily looked around at all of us. Most of the girls seemed confident, but a few looked nervous.

I wasn't sure what I was.

"Your turn," she said. "We'll call up three girls a time, lined up right here. We'll play the music again, and I'll do it at the same time as you while Mrs. Collins scores."

Mrs. Collins called my name for the first round. Of course.

I took a deep breath and pretended once again that this was pretty similar to dance, and I was good at dance.

Mrs. Collins pressed play again, and I kept my peripheral vision on Lily. But I breathed a sigh of relief at the end when I realized I barely needed to follow her.

I'd always been good at memorizing dance routines at my old school. Enough that the coach had almost always placed me in the front row. And now that skill was coming in handy.

Maybe this wouldn't be so bad.

Mrs. Collins even gave me an impressed look.

Then, a few minutes later, Lily began doing back-flips and round-offs.

Ummm….

I shot Rachel a desperate look. Stunts were definitely not my forte. I was nowhere near some of these girls' level.

I'd done tumbling for a while as a kid, but these days, all I did were moves that usually kept me well within range of the ground.

Rachel gave me two thumbs up and a reassuring look before it was her turn to go. Just like that, she nailed three backhandsprings —one more than even Lily had done—plus a split to top it all off.

When it was my turn, I showed Mrs. Collins what I could do. A solid round-off, a decent split, but that was it.

She jotted down something and moved on.

I was sure it couldn't get worse than that, being one of three people there who couldn't land a backhand spring, but up next, we had to do actual cheer stunts.

As in throwing people in the air.

Several of the more experienced girls spotted me. Since I was the smallest person in my group, I got chosen to be the flyer.

I wasn't one to chicken out or break into utter panic, but that was about the closest I'd ever come to it.

I focused on not hyper-ventilating. Before I could

tell Mrs. Collins that it was time for me to go (run) home, though, Rachel pulled me aside.

She could probably see the panic on my face. "Rachel, I can't do this!" I cried. What had I been thinking? Never had I asked myself that question as much as I had today.

The thought of me being launched like a faulty rocket into the air and then coming back down to unsure hands…

I gulped. Goodbye, cruel world.

Okay, maybe I was being a tad over dramatic, but I hardly felt guilty for it.

Rachel took my hands in hers. "We've got you. Don't worry. It looks a lot harder than it actually is. Just keep your whole body rigid. As rigid as you possibly can. And trust us. I can already tell you were made for this."

Trust people I'd only just met this afternoon? SURE OKAY.

And what was that nonsense about being made for something I'd NEVER done before?

She gave my hands a squeeze. "I promise you're gonna be fine."

Mrs. Collins gave a blow of her whistle, and I got in the middle of my small group. Rachel gave me a reassuring smile as I put my right hand on her shoulder and my right foot in her hands. The girls held onto my feet tightly and pushed me up into the air in one swift motion.

Fighting down a fresh wave of panic, my stomach doing more flips than I ever would, I fought to keep my body rigid. Arms at my side. Smiling more out of sheer fear and shock than anything else.

"Told you you could do this! Go for a heel stretch!" Rachel called from down below.

Huh? Did she expect me to figure out what that meant, all while hoping I didn't break my neck?

She called out again. "Lift up your leg! Touch your toe to your hand!"

I finally knew what she was talking about, but I couldn't believe she was asking me to potentially lose my balance and die.

In school.

But for some reason, I thought to myself: what the hay?

May as well go for it, right?

If I'm gonna risk my life out here, I may as well go down attempting a fancy move.

The girls let go of my right foot, and before I could think too much about it, I gritted my teeth hard through my smile and lifted my foot as high as I could.

Thank goodness for all the dance practice because otherwise, I probably would've fallen. It took every ounce of strength in my core and remaining leg to stand steady.

After a couple of seconds, I brought my leg back down.

Rachel's voice somehow reached my already at-capacity brain. "Ready?"

They tossed me up, I gave a small scream, and then I came back down in a basket toss.

The girls stood me back up, and I seriously thought

I would keel over into a heap. Maybe it was the course of adrenaline that kept me on my two feet.

Rachel took one look at me and began laughing uncontrollably. "I've got to hand it to you, Scarlett. I didn't think you could do it, but you rocked it."

I scoffed at her, mouth hanging open and eyes wide.

That just made her laugh harder. "You look like a deer in headlights…but worse."

"You didn't think I could do it?" I demanded.

She shrugged. "I thought there was a good chance you would do okay. But you surprised me. You're a natural flyer."

I scoffed again. "You call that being a natural? I thought I was going to die!"

Mrs. Collins came over. "You didn't tell me you had experience in cheer."

Staring at her in disbelief, I managed to utter, "I don't."

Now it was Mrs. Collins's turn to be a little speechless. "Well, then," she replied. She jotted something down on her clipboard and left.

I turned back to Rachel. "This is not what I thought tryouts were going to be like."

She gave me a knowing smile. "Did I not mention that we're one of the best squads around here?" She winked and began sauntering off.

I noticed several boys coming in from the football field.

"By the way," Rachel said, turning back. Her voice came out low. "Ben over there? He couldn't keep his eyes off of you the whole time you were up there." With a wide grin, she continued walking. "You're welcome."

I could've bottled up the confidence Rachel gave off. That's the type of girl she was. She reminded me of Anne in a lot of ways. How much she made me laugh and smile for one.

But her comment about Ben? Yeah, right.

Making my way to the locker room after everyone else, I eyed the boys milling about the gym.

They looked like they weren't done with practice yet. More like on a break from the heat, and from the looks of it, a grueling practice outside.

My gaze found Ben. He was downing a long swig of water from one of those green plastic Gatorade bottles. Another staple of American high schools everywhere.

He brought the bottle back down and wiped at his mouth with his arm. Then his eyes met mine.

Just like that, I was back to being a giant mess, even from across the gym.

And I couldn't look away. What was wrong with me?

After a couple of seconds, he looked away first, glancing down before his friend came over with something to say.

I grabbed my sweater and continued walking, gaze forward this time, wondering if Ben now thought I was a complete weirdo.

Because around him, I definitely morphed into one. Ugh.

4

RACHEL SAT down with a big grin at lunch, setting her tray down loudly on the table. She looked at me immediately. "Did you check yet?"

"Check what?" I asked, paying more attention to the slice of pepperoni pizza in front of me.

She gave me an exasperated sigh. Nora's mouth turned up at the corner before she went back to checking her phone, and Audrey leaned in, clearly also wondering what Rachel was talking about.

Rachel raised a brow, still staring at me. "Cheer, hello? Mrs. Collins sent out emails at noon?"

Oh yeah.

I pulled out my phone and looked for the email. "I completely forgot. I mean, I didn't want to get my hopes up or anything. With you guys being one of the best squads around and freakin' Rachel here doing about a dozen backflips at tryouts…" My voice faded into nothing as I opened the email and read it.

Why did I see a knowing—and widening—smile on Rachel's face out of the corner of my eye?

I raised my head slowly. After blinking several times and figuring out how to breathe again, I said, "Shut. Up."

Nora snorted. "Okay, Princess Diaries. I'll bite. What's going on?"

I showed her the email, and at the same time, Rachel began screaming.

For some reason, I began screaming too, and then Audrey joined in.

Nora looked at the email. We waited for her to join us, but no go.

She covered her ears. "Yeah, no," she said. "I don't do the girly screams. I'm with you in spirit, though, Scarlett," she finished with a chuckle.

I turned back to Rachel. "I honestly can't even right now. I did not make the squad…"

She nodded. "You totally did! And girl, I'm surprised that you're surprised. I mean, for someone with zero cheer experience…I mean, even for someone with cheer experience, you killed it yesterday! Lily said Mrs. Collins couldn't stop talking about you. She thinks you have a lot of potential, and we could use more fliers."

Me, a flier?

My stomach began doing this weird roiling thing at the thought of that. "I don't know, Rachel. It must have been some sort of a fluke because I'd never been more scared in my life. The more I think about it, the more I realize how lucky I am to not have broken my neck."

Rachel rolled her eyes. "Doubt yourself all you want, but I see how amazing you are. You don't even know it." She smiled, and I couldn't help but do the same.

"You really think so?" I asked.

"I know so," she replied right away. "First football game's in two weeks. Which means we've got a lot of work to do. I'm not kidding when I say we're the best. People go crazy for our half-time routine as much as the football game. Practice starts today after school."

The nerves and worry crept back in. What had I gotten myself into? Then again, I was no stranger to hours of practice. But cheer? This was new territory, and I still wasn't sure how I felt about it.

"Believe me, football games are so much more fun from down in the field than up in the stands." She began eating again.

Nora tossed her hair back. "Yeah, I'll stick to my drums and my fellow band geeks. You guys have fun, though."

Audrey laughed. "I'll stick to the stands and enjoy both of your performances."

Rachel put down her sandwich. "Oh, and one more thing. You'll be assigned a football player by Mrs. Collins. We bake cookies, write encouraging notes on their lockers on game day, that kind of thing."

I eyed Ben across the cafeteria. Say what?

Rachel nudged me with a laugh and went back to her lunch.

Audrey glanced at Ben too. "Sounds like you joined the right extracurricular activity."

I shook my head. "No way."

But the truth was, I couldn't wait to see Ben Garcia in his football uniform underneath the Friday night lights.

And it sounded like I would have a great view.

5

I SCOOPED up some fried rice and vegetables onto a paper plate and joined Mom on the couch.

These kinds of nights were my absolute favorite.

Chinese on the couch in front of the TV.

Catching up on each other's day while watching a classic. Tonight it was Crazy Stupid Love.

It didn't get better than this.

"Mm," Mom said, devouring her dinner. "We should totally re-watch The Office again. I miss Jim."

Mom was completely obsessed with Jim, especially in the later seasons once it was obvious that the actor had started working out.

Couldn't blame her.

"I miss Dwight," I added with a grin.

Ah, Dwight.

I appreciated TV that made me laugh, brought a smile to my face on the lonely days. Like the ones where Mom worked late and came home at bedtime.

"So how's the new job?" I asked.

She nodded and kept her eyes on the TV. "It's good. I like it. The people are nice. The boss isn't a jerk. And I like what I'm doing. A lot, actually."

She turned and gave me a quick smile. "How's school so far? Are you settling in?"

"School's good. I met three girls. Rachel, Audrey, and Nora. They're cool," I said, grabbing some more rice.

"Three friends already?" Mom asked. "Look at you. And your teachers? You like them?"

"Yeah, they're great," I went on. You always had a teacher who was kind of boring and all they did was lecture. Definitely had one of those. Plus the super strict teacher. But that was high school. "My favorite is Mrs. Collins. She teaches Human Anatomy & Physiology. She's fun. Plus she coaches cheer."

Mom seemed a little surprised. "Brains and brawn. Cool."

She had a point. "Totally. You'd like her."

Mom had done cheer in high school, and she'd always wished I would fall in love with it too. She'd given up years ago, though, when I'd fallen for dance instead.

I'd been wanting to share the news with her the past couple of days, knowing how crazy excited she'd be. Another reason I'd gone to tryouts. "So... Jefferson doesn't have a dance team," I began.

She gave me a sad look. "Oh, honey, that's too bad. I'm sorry."

"It's okay," I went on. "Rachel actually does cheer.

They had tryouts the other day…" I took a deep breath, getting ready for what was coming.

But Mom was too busy paying attention to Ryan Gosling on the giant screen in front of us. "I decided to go and… I actually made the squad." I couldn't help but give a little laugh, mostly from disbelief.

I waited for Mom to leap from the couch, scream, hug me, something.

But she'd gotten engrossed in the part with Emma Stone and Ryan Gosling at his apartment or whatever. Doing a stunt of their own.

I turned back to the TV and smiled, waiting for the news to hit her.

In the middle of Emma jumping into Ryan's arms, it hit. "WAIT, WHAT?" she screamed, setting her plate down on the coffee table.

Already taken aback from her reaction, I shut my eyes and braced for the worst to come.

"YOU MADE THE CHEER SQUAD?" she screamed. I peeked at her. Were those actual tears in her eyes? I had definitely underestimated her reaction because… "But that means…YOU TRIED OUT FOR THE CHEER SQUAD?"

The tears came on full-force then. Shock, disbelief, pride, who knew.

Then came the hug, tight enough to hear a few ribs crack. "Oh, honey, I'm so proud of youuuuuu," she cried into my hair. "I always wondered if you had cheer in your blood like me, and you do."

Uh, I didn't know about that.

I made a mental note to stop being such a people-pleaser, but the truth was that cheer did seem kind of exciting.

Being up in the air like that at tryouts...it had been terrifying, but also exhilarating.

And the thought of cheering on Ben—I mean the varsity football team? It sounded like a lot of fun. Something to do other than sit around waiting for Mom to come home from a long day at work.

The more I thought about it, the more I wanted the full high school experience. Friday night football games, cheesy dances in the gym, all of it. I didn't want those experiences to pass me by while I sat at home.

Mom finally let me go. "I can't believe this," she said, her eyes still glittering with tears. "Oh, I can't wait to watch you cheer from the stands. I'm going to have to give you some pointers."

I giggled, trying to picture Mom cheering me on instead of the football team.

That would be her. I made another mental note, one to check any kind of signage she created.

It wouldn't be the first time she did something pretty embarrassing, even if she did have good intentions.

"And we're going to have to celebrate," she went on, the movie now completely forgotten. She began pacing. "I'm thinking mani-pedis, a blowout on the day of your first game, the entire works." She looked at me, grabbed some of my hair. "Oh, I have so much to teach you."

"Mom, it's the cheer squad, not a cult," I joked.

She pursed her lips. "Honey, take it from a cheer veteran. You have no idea," she replied. She gave me one more smile and hug. "Now, tell me exactly how tryouts went."

I told her all of it, how I got picked to be a flyer even though I had no idea what I was doing.

Mom gave a little scream. "I knew it! I was the best flyer on my team. It's in the genes, I'm telling you."

Almost an hour later, Mom began telling me more about what was going on at work.

And it started with her looking kind of nervous. Most of our dinner lay on the coffee table, cold and forgotten. "So the senior vice president really liked the work I did at the previous branch. Apparently, my old boss put in a really good word for me, which is…amazing. Anyway, I've been chosen to lead this super important project. One of our biggest clients. I'm talking a nice enough bonus if it goes well that maybe we can finally take one of our trips?" she finished, still seeming a little on edge.

Now it was my turn to squeeze her non-stop. "Mom, that's great! I can't believe it. It sounds like an incredible opportunity."

"It really is, Scarlett," she went on. "The only catch is that it'll mean quite a few late nights, maybe a few weekends at the office while we take on this project. I mean, it's gotta be our best work. And it's a demanding client. But who knows? In a year or two, I could be a senior manager. Get a really nice pay raise, enough to take lots of our trips. But the next few months might be kinda rough."

I opened my mouth to say something, anything.

Wow, that had been a lot. "The next few months?" I managed.

She scooted closer. "Yeah, honey. Which is why it's perfect that you decided to join cheer. That'll keep you busy, and you'll have time with your friends. And I'm gonna let you pick what trip we take first. How does that sound?"

One of the things we used to do with Dad was take trips around the country, visit historical sites, that kind of thing.

Ever since he'd passed away a couple of years ago, we hadn't done anything like that. But eventually, we'd come up with a vision board, one full of trips Mom and I wanted to take while I was still in high school and college.

Trips to Europe, Asia, Australia, South America. We'd been gathering pictures of places and things we'd wear, the kinds of hotels we'd stay at.

It was another one of our things, a hope that kept us going through dark times.

There had been a lot of dark times. It was part of the reason we'd moved here. For more sunshine. Literally and metaphorically.

A new start, away from the memories that continued to haunt us. As hard as it was to move away from Dad and where he rested, Mom had convinced me that we needed this.

But more than anything, I could see that she did.

Mom scooted a little closer to me on the couch. "Say something, Scarlett." Her voice came out small and a little scared.

Right away, I gave her a smile. "Yeah—it's fine. It'll be fine. I'm really excited for you, Mom."

I wrapped her in a hug. I really was happy for her, but more than anything, I didn't want her to see how crushed a big part of me was. She was everything to me.

More than friends ever could be, and it was hard when it was just me. Home alone with only silence.

The silence brought a lot of sadness and grief with it, even now, no matter how loud I played The Office.

Mom pulled back and met my eyes. "I promise I will always be there for you. I'll make it to at least some of your games. This is just temporary, okay?"

I nodded and pasted on another smile. "I know. I'm not worried. Just promise me you'll kick butt, okay?"

She hugged me again. "Promise."

And I swallowed the frog in my throat.

6

JEFFERSON WENT from new and unfamiliar to slowly becoming normal and routine.

First period, second, then third. Lunch. Another three periods until the final bell and then cheer practice. Every afternoon, the girls marched into the gym to practice stunts and dance routines while the boys went down to the football field to run through plays and prepare for their first game of the season.

With plenty of encouragement from Rachel and Mrs. Collins, I got better at flying. The dance part of the routine was easy enough, but learning to nail a flip in the air?

I landed in a basket toss for the tenth time that afternoon, which meant I was seeing three of Rachel for a second or two.

She grinned. "That one was perfect. Do it just like that."

I stood up. "Thanks. I'm just glad I went with a light lunch today."

Mrs. Collins gave me a pat on the shoulder as she walked by. "Good work today, Scarlett. After just a week's work, you can pass for a complete pro."

Rachel bumped my hip with hers. "What'd I tell you? We are not going to be one of the best this year. We are going to be THE best."

Mrs. Collins blew her whistle, signaling the end of practice, but before I could drag my sweaty self to the locker room, she called us all to her. "Good job today, ladies. First game is days away, but I think we'll be ready to knock everyone's socks off by then."

Lily and a few of the other girls clapped and cheered.

I focused on standing steady.

Mrs. Collins went on. "One more thing and then you're dismissed. Lily has your football player assignments. Each of you will receive the name of a varsity football players. Most of you know the drill, but Lily will explain. Have a good night."

With that, she was off to her office, already making notes and who knows what else on that clipboard of hers. I'd never seen anyone quite as dedicated as Mrs. Collins. It was easy to see how the cheer squad at Jefferson High had evolved into one of the best in the state. Mrs. Collins didn't play. According to Rachel, she'd cheered most of her life. Was practically a legend.

I turned back to Lily, who held a stack of small strips of paper in her hand.

One by one, she began calling out names.

I looked around at the anxious and excited faces. Was it me or was this a big deal?

Rachel went up for her sheet then joined me. "Everyone always hopes to get their crush or at least a cute senior." She looked at the name on her paper. "Not bad."

I glanced at it.

Aaron Garcia.

Was that a slight blush on her cheeks? I opened my mouth to ask her just that, but then Lily called my name.

I grabbed my sheet, read it, and stopped in my tracks.

Benjamin Garcia.

I stood in front of Rachel without blinking for a few seconds before she noticed the expression on my face and practically tore the paper from my hands.

She grinned wide. "You got Ben?"

I glanced around nervously. "Um, say it louder. I don't think the next town over heard you," I said with a nervous laugh.

Because her words had definitely gotten some interesting looks from some of the other girls.

Disappointed looks. Jealous looks.

I'd been working with these girls for the past week, and I'd been surprised at how much nicer they all were than the haughty cheerleaders at my old school.

But obviously, it didn't take much more than a hot football player to bring out some cattiness. I would've been more surprised to not get those looks.

Ben really was a universal crush around here. Great.

Rachel went on smiling.

"What?" I asked. "Are these not assigned randomly?"

She shrugged. "For the most part. Only the captain and Mrs. Collins really know for sure, but it's interesting that you, a newbie, got one of the star players." She winked. "I mean, what are the chances?" She raised a brow. "Or did fate have anything to do with it?"

I shrugged. Part of me suddenly became kind of suspicious but... nah. "Seems to me like a weird coincidence and nothing more. So I've gotta bake him some cookies." I took the paper with Ben's name back.

Rachel put her hands on her hips. "I don't think you understand what this means. It's kind of a big deal to get a star player like Ben. You've really got to go above and beyond. You'll need to talk to him, you'll cheer for him when his name is called at pep rallies and games, that kind of thing. And he might ask you to a party here and there. It's their way of thanking us."

I blinked back at her. Clearly I didn't realize what all of this entailed. "Um, I thought I was joining cheer, not the football support squad. Besides, you said Ben didn't date."

She grinned and shrugged her shoulders. "You never know."

But I was more worried about personally cheering on Ben.

The cheerleaders at my old school didn't do all this stuff. Did they?

Rachel began walking toward the locker room, and I followed her. "We take care of our football players. It might not seem that important, but it makes a big difference in how we come across to other schools, not to mention their own confidence. And we all know boys pretend to be gods out there on that field, but their self-esteem suffers just as much as ours."

I kinda laughed at that. She had a point.

Still, I felt nervous just thinking about making posters for Ben, cheering for Ben, making cookies and having to hand them to Ben.

As thrilling as it would be to be around him, he intimidated me. Every time I saw him in the hallway or in the lunchroom, his gaze slid right past me. And past most girls.

My friends had been right.

He did not date. He hardly even talked to girls. He seemed pretty quiet in general.

Sometimes he laughed or talked to some of the guys around him, but other than that, he kept to himself. Seemed to spend a lot of time in his own head or getting his schoolwork done. Unlike most of the guys on the football team.

I wondered what he was really like, past that cool exterior.

If I was lucky, maybe I'd find out.

7

ON SATURDAY, I woke up to an empty house.

The note and the twenty dollar bill on the kitchen counter, not to mention the lack of the washer and dryer going, gave it away.

Even though it was just me and Mom, she was usually up early, brewing coffee and knocking things off her to do list.

But this morning, the house was eerily quiet, just the hum of the refrigerator to keep me company.

I picked up the note. Mom's messy handwriting said:

Had to go in early. Be back by dinner. No time for grocery shopping so treat yourself today :)

Love, Mom

I checked the time on the stove.

11:13am.

It was practically lunch time.

Between cheer practice and homework, it had been a brutal week. I gave a big yawn.

I might need a nap later.

By the time I showered and got dressed, I was definitely ready to eat.

I lay in bed and looked up local restaurants, in the mood for something other than pizza or takeout.

We only had one car between the both of us, but there were some places not too far. Maybe I could even catch an Uber and go into town for a couple of hours, do some window shopping and get out of this empty house.

Lately, Netflix until Mom came home wasn't enough. Not with all the hours she'd been putting in. I'd hardly seen her all week, and I'd missed her this morning.

I scrolled through a list of places downtown.

A place called Bobby's Cafe caught my eye. Great ratings, the food looked amazing, and it was in a shopping center.

After texting Mom my plans, I called an Uber.

Several minutes later, my phone dinged with a text.

Mom: Text me every 30 min? Glad you're getting to explore!

It would've been a lot more fun with her, but maybe soon.

On my way to Bobby's Cafe, I realized I probably should've asked Rachel, Audrey, or Nora if they were up for some food and shopping.

Duh.

Way better than the thought of me getting out of the house only to be alone elsewhere.

I quickly texted them.

Just as I walked into the cafe, my phone dinged again.

Nora: Sorry, girl. Working today. Rain check?

Audrey: Can't today either. But let's plan something :)

I drooped like a flower but tried to keep my head up. I turned to the menu in front of me.

Bobby's Cafe boasted well over a hundred reviews for a reason. That much was obvious because the place was packed. I found a couple of empty stools at the bar near the kitchen up front.

Then my phone dinged again.

Rachel: Guess what??

Just as I began texting back, I heard her voice.

"Scarlett!"

I spun around. There she was. I couldn't help but laugh at the sight of her.

She already had a couple of shopping bags in tow.

She came in for a hug with an excited shriek. "Talk about great minds. I'm sooo glad you texted me. Lily promised to go shopping with me today and then she had to bail. SATs or something," she said with a roll of her eyes.

I giggled. "I'm glad I texted you too. I've been so bored at home. My mom's been working crazy hours. I had to get out of the house."

Rachel took a seat on the stool next to me, placing her bags on the floor underneath. "Ugh, me too. But I've got the opposite problem. My house gets kind of crazy so sometimes I've got to escape it because of that."

A crazy house. I wondered what that was like. My parents had had trouble conceiving me, and no matter how hard they'd tried, they'd never been able to have another baby. So it had always just been me.

Anne back home had always complained about her sisters, but I'd secretly wished I had a sibling to keep me company, even if they did steal my clothes and favorite snacks.

My stomach growled loudly. I grabbed the menu in front of me. "So are you hungry? Because I'm starving."

Rachel grabbed a menu of her own. "I could eat a horse." She glanced at me. "You picked the perfect spot, by the way. The food here is delicious, and…"

I was about to ask her and what, but before I could, my attention went elsewhere.

Not the sizzling patties on the grill just a few feet away or the crispy French fries being poured into baskets but the guy who'd just walked in from the back. The double doors swung shut behind him, and he was wearing a black uniform and apron, but it may as well have been a runway from the way he carried himself.

Rachel continued, but I hardly heard her voice among the sound of plates being set down on the counter and the buzz of the customers. "And the fact that the eye candy here is so perfect you hardly need dessert. Although the strawberry cheesecake here is to die for."

"Uh huh," I managed, my eyes still locked on Ben.

Could there be a better looking football player in the United States? I'd only lived here and in Massachusetts my whole life, but if I were a betting girl, my money would be on Ben Garcia.

I mean, how had he not been recruited by Disney or

Netflix to star in the next High School Musical or something?

The boy had it all.

Perfectly tousled deep brown hair. A chiseled jaw and defined brows. Topped off with a mouth that gave me goosebumps in that rare moment when it transformed into a smile.

Ben walked past, grabbed a couple of plates, and delivered them all the way down the counter.

I finally tore my gaze away from him, only to find Rachel staring at me with a teasing smile playing on her lips. "Wow, you've got it bad," she said, drawing out that last word.

I scoffed and went back to reading the menu. "I don't know what you're talking about."

So I'd been totally entranced by him for like...ten seconds. It meant nothing.

Nothing whatsoever.

I cleared my throat and continued studying the menu. It wasn't long before something there stole my attention. "Oh, this cajun club sandwich sounds amazing."

Rachel took the bait. "It's one of my favorites. Make sure you ask for Bobby's special sauce on the side for the fries." She made this sound then like just the thought of that had made her die early and go to heaven.

"Welcome to Bobby's," I heard. Before I even put down the menu, I knew who it was. I would recognize that voice anywhere. Ben. "Can I get you guys started with drinks?"

Ben waited for me to say something, but I froze like the total dork I apparently was.

Luckily Rachel stepped in just before it turned weird. "Hey, Ben," she said confidently. Where could I get some of that?

Ben turned toward her. "Hey, Rach. How's it going?"

"Pretty good," she replied, a wide smile on her face. How did she do that? Manage to speak coherently while the hottest guy on earth stood right there? "How's your day going?" Now she turned to me for a second, and I could tell she was wanting me to say something.

Panic filled my insides.

Ben glanced at me too before responding. "You know, work's work. Pretty busy, though, so that's good."

Rachel leaned forward. "So this is Scarlett. She's new to Jefferson and the cheer squad."

I gave him a small wave, immediately wondering how lame that was. "Hi," I squeaked. Okay, why did my voice sound like that??

He gave me a quick wave back. "Hey. Congrats on cheer. I know they don't just take anyone."

He actually sounded kind of impressed. That made me grin. "Thank you."

"How are you liking Jefferson?" he asked. "Sorry I had to run off the other day."

Now Rachel looked intrigued.

"It's okay," I said, my voice finally resembling a normal pitch. "Jefferson's great."

He nodded. "Good." He paused, looking at the menus again. "So…drinks?"

"Um, Coke for me, please," I said.

"Water," Rachel answered. "And we'd love your expert opinion. It's Scarlett's first time here, so we're wondering what you think she should try first." There was that confident smile again.

Ben set down a couple of straws. "You can't go wrong with the Cajun Club or the classic burger. Just remember to ask for—"

"Bobby's sauce on the side," Rachel finished at the same time.

That made Ben laugh a little. "That's right."

Rachel handed him our menus. "Make it two cajun club sandwiches then. No onions for me, please."

He grabbed the menus. "You got it."

And then he was gone, off to put the order in the computer a few feet away.

Rachel nudged me. "Oh my gosh, I think he likes you!"

I glanced in Ben's direction, hoping her voice hadn't carried, but he was busy getting our drinks now. "No way. He was just being nice."

Rachel shook her head. "You don't get it. Ben never talks that much. I can hardly get three words out of him whenever I come in here. And he never smiles either."

"I don't know," I said, my voice trailing off. "He seemed like he was just being nice," I insisted.

Rachel gave me this look like she didn't think so. "I've known Ben since we were kids, and I'm telling you. He's usually all business." She paused then her eyes flashed. "And what's all this 'Sorry, I couldn't stick around' business?"

Twenty minutes later, Rachel and I sat back, completely satisfied. We'd only managed to eat half our sandwiches each, and I was actually sad at the thought of not eating the rest. "I think I just found my new favorite place to eat," I said with a sigh.

"Tell me about it. Bobby's sauce and his deliciously evil fries are the reason I'm gonna gain the freshman fifteen before I'm even a college freshman," Rachel quipped.

I laughed. "Count me in."

Ben came over with some to go boxes and a large slice of cheesecake. We looked at him in surprise when he set it down in front of us with two forks.

Rachel raised a brow. "We didn't order this."

He gave us a quick smile. "I know. It's on the house. Since this is Scarlett's first visit here."

I sat up, never seeing a more perfect image than one of a cute boy handing me cheesecake. "Wow, thank you. Tell Bob I said thanks."

That made him chuckle. "Will do. Enjoy."

He set down our check too and left.

Rachel picked up her fork and began chowing down despite complaining of being super full just a minute ago. "Yeah, he definitely likes you."

I took a bite of cheesecake too, going for a big chunk of graham cracker crust. It was my favorite. "I don't know why you keep saying that."

Rachel glanced at the cheesecake then looked at me. "The boy just brought over free dessert. Which again, is not a thing here. Birthdays, yes. First visit? No." She gave me a wink. "Unless he thinks you're cute, that is."

I went back to eating some more of the cheesecake, but I couldn't help but smile.

Ben was just being nice. No way would he have any reason to like me. Especially not when he supposedly didn't date.

As we boxed up our food, though, I couldn't help but look over at him.

Was it me or had he been looking at me too?

He picked up several empty plates off the counter and went through the black double doors.

As we walked into the first store, Rachel turned to me. "You should've told him that he's your football player this season," she said.

"No, thank you," I replied. "That was awkward enough as it was."

Rachel led me right over to the junior section. "Who knows? Maybe he'll end up being yours in more ways than you think this season."

"Rachel Vasquez," I said, giving her a playful push. "You are the worst."

8

THE FIRST FOOTBALL game of the season rolled around faster than I was ready for.

I'm not sure who was more nervous.

Me or the varsity football coach.

While he paced back and forth during a nail-biting first half, I fought to not throw up at the thought of the upcoming half-time show.

Once again, I asked myself: WHAT HAD I BEEN THINKING?

The beginning of the game had been easy enough, but even that had almost turned into a disaster.

When the guy at the mic announced Ben's name and number, I did a round-off. Round-offs were easy. I could do them in my sleep, but I'd stumbled as I'd landed. Thankfully, everyone had been too busy cheering on our star wide receiver to notice my not-so-great stunt.

Performing was not anything new for me, but this football game had me more anxious than ever. Maybe because pulling off a cheer routine consisting of dance, cheering, and stunts was a whole different ball game.

And while at a ball game!

Before, I'd always performed in front of parents, on stage, before a panel of professional judges.

Tonight, a loud crowd of peers, parents, and who knows who else would be the judges.

Would they cheer us on? Clap? Start booing if I seriously flopped?

My hands went to my roiling stomach. I'd been too nervous to eat before, and I was glad.

The last thing I needed was to throw up on the field in front of everybody. Not the kind of start I wanted at Jefferson.

Rachel came over and handed me a couple of Mentos. "Here. I remember my first half-time show well. These'll settle your stomach. Helps me every time."

I took them and popped them in my mouth. "Thanks."

Lily began the next cheer, and I joined in, pasting a giant minty smile on my face. The crowd must have had well over a hundred, hundred and fifty people tonight. They were loud.

But we were louder.

The sound of instruments practically made the earth shake. Nora, in her band uniform with her drumsticks in hand, gave me a small wave, and I waved back and smiled.

A few minutes later, the whistle went off, signaling the end of the first half. I glanced at the scoreboard. We were down two points.

The boys came in from the field. I found Ben once his helmet came off. He shook the wet hair away from his forehead. Was it me or did time slow down when he was around?

Sweat dripped down his forehead. He wiped it away with his forearm. Pretty soon, he was following the rest of the team into the locker room. I forgot to blink for a few seconds, admiring the feat of engineering and ingenuity that was a pair of football pants.

I snapped back to attention. Lily screamed something about getting out there and in formation.

Uh oh. That's right. The halftime show.

I ran beside Rachel, who gave me a thumbs up. "Break a leg!"

With a half laugh, half cry, I replied, "I hope not!"

That made her cackle, but she quickly became quiet as she found her spot. I found mine in the row behind her.

Head down, hands at my side.

The crowd in front of us went from a loud buzz to a quiet murmur.

The last thing that flashed through my mind was that at least the football team was too busy reviewing the playbook to be out here watching us. Knowing that Ben wasn't watching definitely helped my chances of not landing on my butt or face at some point.

The music boomed through the stadium, and I moved, not letting myself think too much. Thinking too much made me mess up. So instead, I moved with the music. Sometimes dancing, sometimes chanting at the top of my voice, and sometimes pumping my fist into the air.

The first stunt was coming up. I prepared myself mentally and then it was time. The girls pushed me up in one fluid motion. My smile grew wide at the sound of the crowd screaming for us. My right leg went up at the same time as the girls to either side of me.

More screams.

I came back down, and we continued moving, dancing, screaming.

Yes, this was scarier, crazier, riskier, but somehow, it was also ten times more exhilarating than dance.

I got ready to go up again, but this time, I didn't just go up. I flew. I kept my legs and head tucked in, wanting to scream like I was on a rollercoaster but stifling the urge.

Especially when I fell back down.

Before I could even wonder if the girls would be there to catch me, they had.

Not perfectly, but good enough.

Rachel met my eyes for a split second and winked before moving to her next position.

At the end of the show, the crowd screamed and cheered like we'd just scored another touchdown.

Afterward, in the locker room, Rachel gave me a slap on the rear. "See, and you were worried! You killed it out there!"

I gave her a hug. "Thanks! And thank you for not letting me fall to my death," I said with a laugh. Then I took a long and deep breath. "Wow, that was awesome."

"Right?" She bumped her hip with mine. "We'd

never let you fall to your death, silly. Broken leg, though? Maybe."

I bumped her back. "Oh gosh."

She winked again. "Kidding."

We took a break, got a job well done speech from Mrs. Collins, and headed back out onto the field.

The boys were already there.

Rachel must have seen me glancing around because she leaned into my ear. "Number 28 is right over there," she said, nodding her head in the opposite direction I'd been looking.

Sure enough, Ben was there, chugging down some Gatorade. But I tried to play it cool. Putting my hands on my hips, I said, "I was just admiring the team."

Rachel cackled again. "I know what you were admiring."

I couldn't help it. I laughed out loud with her.

Then I wiped the sweat from my brow, fanning myself.

"Here," Rachel said, handing me some of her sports drink. "We've got another half to go."

Another thing about cheer? It was a lot more grueling than I could've imagined.

We cheered through another touchdown from the opposite team.

The crowd cheered and screamed for Jefferson, but things weren't looking good.

At least until we got an interception.

I knew enough about football to know what that was. During the second down, our quarterback managed to make a pass just before getting hit by the other team's elephant-sized defender.

The crowd groaned in worry for him, but we all kept our gaze on the ball arcing through the air. Number 28 ran to meet the ball, but he had two defenders on his tail.

He wasn't gonna make it…

Ben jumped, landed on his side, and rolled.

The crowd erupted into screams.

It was easy to see why. They were just twenty yards from the end zone.

During the next down, Jefferson scored a touchdown.

We did our special touchdown cheer, and I got thrown into the air again.

Our team needed one more touchdown, though, if we were going to win this game.

I checked the time on the clock and saw the coach doing the same. Just twelve minutes left.

The boys continued playing their hearts out, and the girls continued cheering.

With five minutes left on the clock, Jefferson managed to intercept the ball again. This time, though, they made it all the way to the end zone.

"Touchdown for Jefferson!" the speakers boomed.

I flew into the air again.

Finally, the whistle blew for the last time. The boys all ran onto the field, screaming and jumping. Lily gave us a wave, and we did the same.

Rachel found number 29, whose jersey also said Garcia. It was Aaron, Ben's brother.

She gave him a big hug, and I noticed the way he hugged her back. Like he'd been waiting all night to do it.

I smiled and turned away, scanning the crowd and refusing to admit to myself that I was searching for Ben.

Ah, there he was.

Speaking to the coach, his helmet still in his hand. Had that uniform been tailor-made for him or was he just born to rock a football uniform?

The rest of the team continued to mill around, laughing and talking. Several parents joined us on the field, finding their player and going in for hugs.

It had been a good game, a good night.

I ached to have someone to talk to, but Rachel was still talking to Aaron, and I didn't want to be a third wheel.

Mom had wanted to come out tonight and see me perform my first half-time show, but an urgent and last-minute deadline meant she was still at the office.

My gaze went to Ben again. He was on his way back to the locker room, his head down.

Part of me wanted to run up to him and congratulate him on a great game, but I was way too chicken to do that.

So I went over to Rachel instead.

She turned to me and smiled. "There you are. We're all going out to eat. Probably Bobby's Cafe. Are you in?"

I nodded. "Sure. I just need to check in with my mom."

"Cool," Rachel replied. She linked her arms with

mine and Aaron's. "Because I could go for a large order of fries and a chocolate milkshake."

"Anyone else coming?" I asked, also being too chicken to ask specifically about Ben.

"Oh, I'm sure the entire football team and cheer squad will be there. It's kind of our thing on the nights we have home games," she replied. "By the way," she stopped. "This is Aaron. Aaron, Scarlett. She's new this year."

Aaron held out his hand. "Nice to meet you, Scarlett."

I shook his hand and grinned. "Same. You guys played great tonight. Good game."

He smiled back. "Thanks."

Like his brother, he seemed kind of soft-spoken and quiet. They even looked kind of alike, but Aaron's eyes were hazel instead of green and he wore his hair differently. Ben was also taller, but both brothers had a knack for wearing a football uniform like it was made for them.

"Do all of you play football?" I asked as we resumed walking. "Your brothers, I mean."

He chuckled. "No. Ben and I do, and our youngest brother does too. But not Cade and Drake."

Cade and Drake. Huh.

I counted in my head. "So there's…five of you?" I asked, definitely sounding surprised.

He chuckled again. "Yep. And yes, we get that a lot."

Rachel gave me a knowing smile, probably guessing exactly what I was thinking.

Five brothers? Were they all as handsome as Ben and Aaron?

Something told me the answer to that question was a resounding yes.

But as handsome as the other four brothers might be, my heart was set on the one I couldn't have: Ben Garcia.

I was in trouble.

9

BECAUSE THE BOYS had crushed the first football game, Lily insisted we show up to school on Monday with something special.

The group chat pinged with so many messages on Sunday that I could hardly keep up.

Meanwhile, Mom finally had a day off, and we'd decided to order in, catch up on laundry while watching the latest rom-coms, and just be kinda lazy in general. Plus she was begging me to give her the play-by-play from Friday night.

My phone dinged again. It was Rachel suggesting brownies or cookies as a treat for the boys.

I gave that a thumbs up. Her idea was better than the one Lily was suggesting, which was to show up on Monday with custom hand-painted t-shirts.

No, thanks. Between laundry, homework, and watching Noah Centineo on our large flat-screen, I wasn't about to leave the couch to head to the arts and craft store across town on a Sunday afternoon.

Apparently, most of the squad agreed to baked goods.

Baked goods were easy.

My mom and I had frozen cookie dough in the freezer all the time.

Just as Noah's beautiful smile made its appearance on screen, my phone dinged a few more times.

I glanced at the steady stream of incoming messages.

Something about a spreadsheet with something.

But the gist was we had to bake a dozen cookies or half a dozen brownies for our assigned player by tomorrow.

Plus something about doing a cheer for them before homeroom.

Got it.

I went back to my main priority: Noah.

And telling Mom about the second half of the game on Friday plus hanging out after. It had actually been a lot of fun. More fun than I'd had in a long time, AND Ben had been there.

I'd come home exhausted but happy.

After the movie was over, I got up, put away my laundry and books, and headed to the kitchen.

Mom followed me, her laptop in tow. "Whatcha doing?" she asked.

She sat down at the counter, plopping down onto a barstool.

I pulled out the cookie dough.

"Ooh, good idea," she said excitedly, clapping her hands.

But there were just enough cookies to cobble

together a dozen. Ben would get a nice mix of peanut butter, double chocolate chip, and good old oatmeal raisin.

The oatmeal raisin were our diet cookies…

"Sorry," I said. "I've gotta make these for Ben tomorrow. We'll be lucky if we have a couple of extra cookies left over."

Mom pouted. "Aww, okay. I guess I'll settle for a cookie. Probably don't need more than that anyway between all the takeout I've had this week."

"Me too," I said, preheating the oven and grabbing a cookie sheet.

The next morning, I walked into Jefferson with a Ziploc bag full of cookies baked to perfection, along with a congratulatory note taped on the outside and a big and bright BLUE number twenty-eight.

I yawned and looked for Rachel, Audrey, or Nora. Mom and I had stayed up way too late watching funny movies. Worth it, though.

My phone pinged with a text message, and I switched it to vibrate before reading the incoming message.

Rachel: Where are you? Squad meeting in the hallway by the gym.

Oops.

Is that what the twenty new group messages this morning had been about?

I scurried toward the gym.

A couple of minutes later, I was there—and completely out of breath. I shoved my things in my locker and joined the rest of the squad. We'd worn our cheer tops along with our favorite pair of jeans.

The morning announcements began, and the first thing the principal said over the loud speakers?

"Congratulations to our boys varsity football team. They won their first game of the season on Friday night in an outstanding victory against Chestnut Mountain," he said, sounding as proud as if we'd just been declared the national champions of football.

The entire squad cheered, and the boys made their way down the hallway in a loud pack. Several students cheered or high-fived.

Almost as an after thought, the principal added in a monotone voice, "And a great job to our cheerleaders, who pulled off an amazing half-time show."

We all dispersed, but the boys continued soaking in the love and attention for a few more minutes.

Rachel found Aaron and handed him several frosted brownies and a nice number twenty-seven sign for his locker.

I looked around for Ben, not realizing when I'd been baking these cookies last night that I'd have to actually go up to him and talk to him.

Easier said than done, that's for sure.

I made my way through the crowd of student athletes, regular students, and teachers trying to get everyone to homeroom.

There he was, standing at his locker, grabbing his books.

I blew out a breath, ran my hand through my hair, and made my way over.

Just a few feet before reaching him, I opened my mouth only to realize I had no idea what to say.

Hi? Hello? Hey? Good morning?

Here, take some cookies.

Oh yeah, good job on Friday.

No, I needed a minute to think about what to say without stuttering out incoherent sentences again.

I spun around, only to hear a cool, "Hey."

My eyes widened, and I froze.

Um…

I turned around slowly, the bag of cookies still in my hands.

Ben glanced down at them then at me. "Scarlett, right?"

I nodded. "Hey. Yeah, that's me."

That's me??

Really?

I stuck out my hand, practically shoving the cookies in his perfect face.

His mouth twitched a little, like he was holding back a grin.

"Uh, these are for you," I said, trying to recover and making a mental note to speak first and then hand him the cookies. "Great job on Friday night," I added, finally sounding kind of like a normal person.

He took the cookies, his fingers brushing mine and sending my insides into a tizzy. "Thank you." He gave me a small smile this time. "I heard you guys killed it at half time."

"Thanks," I replied with a smile of my own.

His smile grew a little wider. "And it was really cool

how you flew into the air every time we made a touch-down. You guys are really good."

My smile ached to reach cheddar-level cheesy, but I kept it under control. For the most part. "Thank you," I managed.

We stood there for a second, neither of us really knowing what to say next.

"See you at the next game," I said. "I hope you like the cookies."

He held up the bag for a second. "Thanks."

I spun around in a flash, itching to find Rachel.

Or at least get out of the ten-foot radius of Ben that drove me a little crazy.

The bell rang for first period, but I knew Mrs. Collins would excuse me for being a little late since I was on the squad. I found Rachel exiting the girls' bathroom.

"Mission accomplished," I told her.

She joined me as we walked. "I was going to ask you what kind of cookies you made for Ben. Like, did you find a recipe online? I always opt for brownies just because it's easier with the peanut allergy they have—"

I stopped dead in my tracks and took her by the shoulders. "Rachel, what peanut allergy? Tell me you're joking."

She blinked back at me, not looking like she was joking in the slightest. "Didn't you look at the spreadsheet?"

I shook my head. "Not really. I thought it was just a list of who got what player and stuff."

She nodded. "And it lists other important stuff, like injuries and allergies."

My hands came to my mouth. After a second, my voice came out in a croak. "How allergic is he to peanuts?"

Now Rachel's face turned white. "Deadly."

I nodded slowly, like this was just a regular piece of non-life-threatening information. "Okay. What homeroom is he in?"

"Chavez," she replied, somewhere between calm and utterly panicked.

Before I could even ask her where the heck that was, she added, "Around the corner. Right hand side."

I didn't stick around to see what else she said after that because I was too busy high-tailing to Mr. Chavez's classroom.

Not to mention imagining how much the football coach, the football team, and the entire school would hate me after they found out I'd killed their star football player.

I pictured handsome Ben's face puffing up after taking a bite of those cookies. Then his throat swelling up...

Was it too late to ask Mom to transfer to another branch, preferably several states away?

Tears filled my eyes as I rounded the corner and saw the sign hanging from the ceiling that read CHAVEZ.

Just a couple doors down.

The door was still open.

I practically came to a screeching halt in the doorway, scanned the class for that familiar face.

There.

First row.

Standing in front of a guy I recognized from the football team.

Reaching into the bag for a cookie.

Then that cookie going straight for his mouth.

No!

I had no idea if I screamed just inside my head or out loud too.

It all happened so fast and yet so terribly slowly.

I ran and tackled Benjamin Garcia straight to the ground.

Landing right. On. Top. Of. Him.

His green eyes stared up at me, his mouth hanging slightly open in utter shock.

I had no idea where that cookie landed, but it was no longer in his hand.

Neither was the bag.

He glanced around for a second, like he wasn't sure what the protocol was for a cheerleader tackling him to the ground and then staying there, completely frozen. "Um, are you okay?" he asked awkwardly.

I came back to my senses then. Scrambled to my feet and offered him a hand up. "I am so sorry. Are you okay?"

That's when I heard the snickers and laughs erupt all around us.

A few people even had their phones out.

I fought the urge to run away and instead pulled Ben up to his feet as best I could pull up a built varsity football player.

Ben began laughing a little. "I think I'm okay. Nothing broken, I think." He touched the back of his head. "Although my head is a little tender."

I covered my face with my hands, completely mortified. Mortified like I'd never been in my sixteen and a half years. "I am so sorry."

Glancing around the room, I wondered how much more embarrassing this would be if I cried too. Because the tears were definitely threatening to spill over.

Why was it that tears did that in public, precisely when we needed very much NOT to cry?

He pulled me aside and stood so that he blocked me from most people's view—and cameras.

Just about everyone got the hint and went back to what they'd been doing.

I swallowed and took a deep breath, blinking away the tears.

The teacher walked in then but obviously hadn't noticed what had just gone down in his classroom because he carried a stack of freshly copied worksheets to his desk and began calling roll.

I chanced a glance at Ben, who looked like he was holding back a giant grin instead of tears. "It's okay," he said. "I'm just wondering if you're okay."

Maybe in a thousand years, long after I'd graduated from Jefferson. I nodded. "I think so."

Ben chuckled a little. "So is there a reason you decided to tackle me? Or…" His voice trailed off.

Right, he had to be wondering what kind of crazy I was to do what I had just done.

Goodness, how to begin. I exhaled. "Um, I kind of didn't realize you had a really bad peanut allergy, and…"

I nodded toward the cookies on the floor. "Those probably would've killed you."

"Ah," he replied, nodding in understanding. "I see. So you just saved my life, after almost killing me."

A smile finally played on my face. "Well, when you put it that way…" It didn't sound so bad.

Ben began laughing pretty hard then.

The sound of it made butterflies swarm my stomach and my smile reach my eyes.

Ben picked up the cookie and the bag and threw them in the trash. "It's okay. I wasn't looking forward to eating those at all," he said with a quick wink.

Was it me or was the room tilting a little?

I blinked and regained my balance.

The bell rang, signaling the start of first period.

I had to go.

I took a step back. "I'll have to make you some more, ones you can actually eat without risk of death."

He grinned. "Looking forward to it."

I turned around to leave, giving him a small wave.

"And Scarlett?" he called.

I faced him again. "Yeah?"

Now Mr. Chavez headed to the front of the room, giving me this look like he was quickly realizing I didn't belong in his class.

"Thanks for not killing me," he said, laughing again. "Really would've put a damper on the next game."

10

AUDREY, Nora, and Rachel wouldn't let me hear the end of the cookie fiasco all week.

On Saturday night, after another victory for the football team, they came over to my house for a sleepover.

Rachel and Nora re-enacted me tackling Ben for the tenth time that evening. Rachel practically body slammed Nora onto my bed. Nora pretended to choke and cough something up. Audrey just about peed her pants laughing

I rolled my eyes but smiled. "If I would've known that this would just be five hours of you guys laughing at me, I never would've invited you all," I teased.

The truth was that I loved their company. They made life at Jefferson, in this town, so much fun.

Rachel wiped actual tears off her face. "I just can't believe you came this close to killing your crush and Jefferson's star football player. I thought this kind of thing only happened in Netflix movies."

"Ha, ha, ha," I replied sarcastically. "Funny you say that because Netflix called this morning with a movie deal. I'm set to make big bucks, and I'm not sharing the money with any of you."

Rachel feigned a hurt expression, Nora hit me with a pillow, and Audrey fake gasped.

As much as they loved poking fun at me, I wouldn't trade these girls for anything.

Anna had been my best friend for years, and we still texted. I'd always love her.

But Audrey, Nora, and Rachel had become friends like no other in a matter of a couple of weeks.

We went back to doing each other's make up while listening to Ariana Grande's latest hits. Nora was an expert at smoky eyes while Rachel knew how to do the perfect beach waves in our hair.

We stood in the front my body-length mirror and posted pictures on Instagram.

"Wow," Nora said. "We look like Bratz dolls."

"I know," Rachel said. "Don't you love it?"

Nora snorted. "Yeah."

For dinner, we ordered in from my favorite Chinese place. Mom came home from work and joined us for a movie. She insisted we doll her up too before yawning and heading to bed looking like she was ready for the runway.

"Your mom is so cool," Audrey told me. "I wish my mom was more laid-back."

"Thanks," I replied. "I like what we have, for sure."

After that, we made cookies and piled ice cream on top before heading back to my room.

Rachel spooned some dessert into her mouth along with the rest of us.

My eyes practically rolled to the back of my head at the taste of the still warm cookie and the cool chocolate ice cream.

"Okay, we need to do this like every week," Nora commented.

I nodded my head.

Rachel scoffed. "Not if we want to fit into our cheer uniforms in a month."

I giggled. "Yeah, you're probably right." I remembered what we'd said before. "Freshman fifteen."

She laughed. "Freshman twenty-five at this rate." But like me, she took another delicious bite.

After a little while, her gaze landed on the picture on my nightstand.

In it, I stood between my mom and dad. It had been my last birthday before he'd passed away. The three of us looked so happy in that moment, not realizing how few days we had before Dad left us forever.

I knew she would ask about him before she even opened her mouth.

Rachel's voice came out low and soft. "What happened?"

I set down my bowl carefully on the floor beside me, trying to decide how I wanted to talk about this. "Um, that's my dad. He, um, passed away a few years ago. Car accident."

My voice broke a little toward the end so I stopped there. It was still hard to talk about him, both for me and Mom.

His death had crushed us, shaken us to the core.

Almost killed Mom, which in turn, had almost killed me.

Audrey put her arm around me. "I'm really sorry, Scarlett."

Nora put down her ice cream too. "I can't even imagine not having my dad."

Rachel nodded. "He seemed like a really good dad. I can tell just from looking at this photo."

I nodded and managed to say, "He was."

Just like that, the tears came. A sob escaped from my chest before I got myself back under control.

All three girls wrapped their arms around me. I closed my eyes and let them.

After a minute, they pulled back.

Rachel looked at me with guilt in her eyes. "Sorry I brought it up. I bet it's still really hard."

I wiped the tears away. "It's okay."

I gave her another hug.

It was then that I knew Audrey, Rachel, and Nora really had become my friends.

I'd been vulnerable and raw with them, and they'd been there for me, a girl they'd just met a few weeks ago. "You guys are the best," I said. "I'm really glad we moved here."

Not just for the fresh start, but for the amazing friends I'd already found.

11

"YOU SHOULD TOTALLY GO UP and talk to him," Audrey said at lunch. We sat at our usual table.

I shook my head. "No, I don't think so. I'd rather not risk humiliation seeing as how I just moved here." I paused, pretending to think. "Oh, wait. I forgot. I've already humiliated myself at this school." I half scoffed, half laughed.

And yet somehow, I'd survived.

Thank goodness.

"Exactly," Nora chimed in. "What do you have to lose?"

Rachel quirked a brow at me like she knew Nora was right.

"Let's see," I said. "My dignity. Nothing much."

Audrey laughed. "That's the spirit."

Ben sat a few seats away from everyone else at his table. He was busy doing some sort of assignment. Every once in a while, someone would say something to him and he'd respond or laugh. Join in the conversation for a minute and then go back to his homework.

I turned to the girls again. "Yeah, I have no reason, absolutely no reason, to go over there and talk to him. I'm just the girl who almost fed him killer cookies, remember?"

Nora sputtered out a little of the water she'd been drinking. She slid back in her seat and wiped her mouth. "I'm sorry," she said, laughing pretty hard.

You'd think the whole ordeal had just happened yesterday and not last week.

She went on laughing, making Rachel and Audrey laugh too. "I just... every time I picture you running..." She erupted in laughter again, so much that she couldn't talk or hardly breathe. "And... crashing headfirst into him..." She laughed and fanned herself. "Ooooh," she said, taking deep breaths. "I'm okay. Continue."

I just stared at her like, "Seriously?"

But I knew they were (mostly) laughing with me, not at me.

Rachel came in closer. "Is it true that you're basically killer cookie girl to Ben now? I mean, previously, you were cute new girl, whatever..." She paused, turned mostly serious. "My point is... you are now seriously on his radar. And that's what counts."

She looked at me like she'd just said the most genius thing in the world.

I stared back at her much like Stanley would in The Office.

She nudged me. "Come on. Go up there and

just say hi. Ask him if he liked the new batch of cookies you gave him!" She waited for me expectantly.

"I don't know," I said. Sure, Ben had been nice enough after the whole incident, even given me what could've almost passed as a smile in the hallway yesterday…

But just go up and talk to him?

That had never been my style.

Knowing me, I'd start sputtering half-words everywhere before bailing.

Audrey picked at her food. "You know what you can do is go up to him and ask him something about the homework that's due later."

I thought about that, actually considered it. "Hmm, the homework approach."

That could work. Maybe.

Nora smiled. "Rachel and Audrey are right. You totally should go and talk to Ben."

I couldn't help but grin. "Really?" I asked, pretty convinced now.

"Oh yeah," Nora went on. "Mostly because I want to see what happens, but yeah."

We began laughing, and I shook my head. "You are terrible."

She smiled proudly.

I looked at Ben one more time. "Maybe I can ask him about the cookies, maybe mention the game on Friday," I said, trying to sound confident.

Rachel patted my shoulder. "There you go. Now go up there and talk to him."

She urged me on, and I stood up. Took a deep breath.

I got this, I told myself.

Just a quick hello, maybe ask about the homework and then mention the game, then I'd be off.

Completely cool and casual.

I began walking over there. And I walked like I never had before.

Shoulders back, head held high, ready to smile, maybe toss the hair back.

Ben hadn't noticed me yet—he was busy scribbling away in his notebook—but he would in a few seconds.

Then, just when I thought he was looking up to find me, his gaze slid to someone else.

Another girl cut me off—ACTUALLY CUT ME OFF—and walked right up to him.

She took a seat next to him and tossed her hair so hard that I almost puked a little.

I stopped dead in my tracks.

"Ben!" she said. "I just wanted to ask you about the math study guide. I'm having such a hard time with this one problem, and I know math is like your best subject." There it was. The million dollar smile and batting of the lashes.

I stood there, frozen in place, wishing I could make my limbs move.

But it was like my brain had decided this was too unbelievable to be real. I had to watch.

Ben flicked his eyes between the assignment in front of him on the table, this girl, and the rest of the cafeteria. "Oh, hey…"

"Hannah," she replied, leaning her head to the side a little.

"I actually don't have the math study guide with me," Ben said, shuffling a few papers as he talked.

Was it me or had he just hidden the math study guide underneath his science homework?

He went on. "But if you talk to Justin, I think he has it done already." He stood up.

"Oh," Hannah said, the disappointment clear on her face. "Okay. Thanks."

She slinked off, and Ben walked off with his binder and books.

Finally, I spun around and scampered back to my table like I had just escaped another major humiliation.

Because, apparently, I had.

As soon as I sat down, the girls and I crowded around each other and began laughing.

"Oh my gosh!" Audrey cried out.

"Did you see that?" Rachel told Nora.

I covered my mouth with my hands. "Yeah, not doing that ever again!"

That had been a close one.

Ben was cute, but I didn't want to be another Hannah to him.

That had not been the right approach.

Maybe there was no right approach.

All I knew was that I didn't want to be the one to find out all the wrong ones.

I'd faced enough humiliation at Jefferson already.

12

SEVERAL DAYS LATER, the final bell rang, dismissing everyone.

Half the class left for home in a blur while I finished writing down the homework assignment in my student planner.

Rachel rolled her eyes. "Just take a picture of it like a normal person," she teased.

I kept on writing. "I like writing things down and crossing them out when they're done," I replied, knowing how dorky that made me sound.

And being completely okay with that.

Rachel stood up and put on her backpack. "Okay, geek. See you at practice. I've gotta go talk to the math teacher about the quiz tomorrow."

"Talk to ya later," I called after her.

I finished writing down the history assignment and stood up to put my books in my bag.

With my back to the door, I didn't even notice Ben

come in until he was already at Ms. Wilson's desk a few feet away.

Several students remained in the classroom, just hanging out and getting ready to leave.

I hesitated for a moment, wondering what Ben was doing there.

We only had one class together, and it was English.

And thank goodness because it was hard enough to focus as it was without him in the same room.

Ms. Wilson's voice reached me where I stood, pretending to look for something in my bag. "...your grade on the latest paper. It counted for fifteen percent of your grade, and because you got a D, it's brought your grade in the class just below passing. I'm afraid you can't play on the football team until your grade in this class is up to par."

I didn't need to turn around and look at Ben to know how disappointed he had to be.

I hardly knew him, but even so, I could see how much he loved football.

Ben asked Ms. Wilson something about re-doing the paper and turning it in before the next game.

Ms. Wilson paused. "I don't normally do this kind of thing, Ben, but you've always been a good student and I know how much you have on your plate. If you can re-do this paper and get at least a B, that should get you passing again. But the next game is only three days away. Are you sure that's enough time? I don't want you getting another failing grade because you didn't have enough time to produce the work needed for a B."

"I can do it," Ben replied quickly. "Thank you, Ms. Wilson."

With that, he left again, taking his paper. I watched him exit the classroom.

I glanced at Ms. Wilson, who'd gone back to grading, thinking about what I'd just seen.

A crazy idea popped into my head, and before I could second guess myself too much, I grabbed my book bag and ran to catch up to Ben.

His long legs and long strides meant I was practically out of breath by the time I reached him down the hall.

"Ben!" I called.

He stopped and turned around. I could still see the worry and disappointment on his face, but it quickly morphed into that serious neutral expression he wore most of the time. "Oh, hey," he replied.

"Hey," I replied, breathing kinda hard.

Ben looked around for a couple of seconds like he wasn't sure what else to say.

Oh, right. I needed to tell him something.

Which all of a sudden, I wasn't so sure about, but it was too late now. "So, uh, I didn't mean to eavesdrop back there," I began. The more I thought about it, the more I realized how nosy I sounded.

"But you did," he finished for me.

He seemed a little mad but mostly embarrassed. I could tell from the way he wouldn't make eye contact. Somehow, this felt worse than tackling him to the ground.

Hopefully, what I was going to say next would save

me instead of making this situation completely morti-fying for the both of us.

"Um, the reason I say all of this is because I thought maybe I could help you re-write your paper so you can get your grade back to passing and play in the next game."

Ben furrowed his brow, like he was trying to under-stand what I'd just said.

Like that had been the last thing he'd been expecting me to say.

Like maybe he wondered how much help I could actually be.

"You could help me get a B?" he asked.

I nodded. "History has always been my best subject. I always ace it."

Now it was my turn to look away briefly, hoping he didn't ask me how or why I was so good at history.

But he didn't.

Instead he took a step closer. "You'd help me, then?" He paused. "Why would you do that?"

I shrugged and met his eyes, laughed a little. "I figure it's the least I could do after I almost killed you. And gave you a concussion."

Now he laughed a little. Boy, I loved it when he smiled wide like that. I fought to keep myself composed instead of melting into a puddle like I usually did. "You didn't almost kill me," he replied. "And my head," he added, touching the same spot from the other day, "is fine."

I put my hands on my hips. "You were about to take a big bite of that cookie, which would have...you know," I finished lamely, not wanting to describe to him how his face would've puffed up and his throat would've done the same, and he would've suffocated in a matter of minutes.

He brought his backpack around and unzipped a small pocket. Then he pulled out an EpiPen. "True. But I probably would've been fine. All of my teachers and most of my friends know about this. And now you do too, in case you ever accidentally feed me killer cookies again."

I lifted my index finger. "Noted. Glad it didn't just come down to me, you know, barreling into you to make sure you didn't eat that contaminated cookie."

He laughed again and put away the EpiPen. He pulled out his paper. Then he looked at me.

I immediately lamented the fact that he was no longer giving me that wide smile.

"So," he said, handing me his paper. "When can we start?"

13

ONE AWESOME BENEFIT of tutoring Ben Garcia?

Free burgers and fries at Bobby's Cafe.

Audrey had hinted that Ben led a busy life. School, football, work, homework, keeping an eye out for his brothers.

She lived next door to them.

So instead of meeting at the library or at his house, we met at Bobby's Cafe during his breaks and after he got off work.

I popped a fry into my mouth while Ben finished wiping down the bar in front of me. It was a slow night, with it being stormy and rainy outside, so we had plenty of time to work on his paper. "If I had known that I'd be getting free food out of this, I would've offered to help you on that paper back when Ms. Wilson first assigned it."

Ben smiled. "Noted. Unlimited fries are a small price to pay in exchange for a passing grade in Ms. Wilson's class."

I smiled back. "Did you say unlimited?"

Freshman twenty-five, here I come.

Her class wasn't the kind where you could pay attention here and there and pass. She took social studies seriously. With his schedule, I could see how Ben was struggling to keep up.

After setting the dirty rags in a designated bucket on the floor behind the counter, Ben came around and took a seat beside me.

I turned toward him, showing him his marked up paper. During the past twenty minutes, I hadn't just been eating free fries, I had also read through his paper and taken copious notes on what he needed to fix and how, even pulling examples from our online textbook.

Ben took one look at it all and raised a brow. "So you can do cheer stunts and you're smart?"

I giggled, feeling my cheeks turn warm. "I'm good at social studies. Just don't ask me to do a trig problem."

He pulled out his laptop, and I did the same. We got to work via Google Docs, only taking quick breaks so that Ben could tend to customers here and there, ringing them up or refilling drinks.

By closing, we'd made huge headway.

"This is great," Ben said in disbelief. "This may actually earn a B."

I laughed a little. "Don't sound so surprised."

He turned to me, and I realized then how close our faces were.

Maybe he did the same because his eyes flicked down to my mouth for like half a second before coming back up.

"Thank you," he said, standing up. "For coming all the way down here and helping me make this essay an actual essay."

"Free food helps," I interjected with a grin.

He smiled back, and I quickly glanced away.

Then I closed my laptop and stood up too. "Happy to help. Another session or two like tonight, and that should do it."

"Really?" he asked, exhaling. "I don't know how I'll ever repay you."

"Are there enough fries in the world?" I quipped, really enjoying the fact that I could now act like a normal human being around Ben.

Then he smiled again, and I once again threatened to melt.

The restaurant stood empty. Just us and a single cook in the back, cleaning up the kitchen.

Ben eyed him. "I should help. But let me walk you to your car, at least."

I whipped out my phone. "Actually, I'm taking an Uber."

A few minutes later, when the app let me know the Uber was just about there, Ben did walk me out, the umbrella in his hand covering us both.

I shivered from the cold and couldn't help but notice how handsome he looked even in his Bobby's Cafe uniform. Something about the apron around his waist. Or maybe the biceps that peeked out from his sleeves.

The Uber pulled up.

"Well," I said. This is me."

When he opened the door for me to get in, I about passed out, but I kept it together.

"Uh, thank you again. Um, let me know when you make it home?" he asked, sounding a little unsure.

I opened my mouth to reply and then remembered that I didn't have his number and vice versa.

Taking what felt like the biggest risk in my life, I unlocked my phone and pulled up a new message. "Okay. Want to put in your number?" I asked, hating how my voice sounded. "You know… so I can let you know."

He took my phone kind of awkwardly, my gaze anywhere but on him while he tapped away.

Count on awkward situations to make you aware how long a few seconds can take.

He handed me back my phone. "Here," he said, taking a step back and giving me a wave. "Good night, Scarlett."

At some point, I realized he'd shut the door and the Uber driver was on his way to my address.

Good night, Scarlett.

Ben's words, the way he looked at me, played in my head on a loop.

When I got home, I rushed to my room, screaming a quick, "I'm home!" to Mom before closing my bedroom door.

I pulled up my messages.

Ben had sent one to himself, a waving hand emoji.

I began tapping out a message to him, repeatedly erasing and then typing something else.

Finally I settled on…

Scarlett: Made it home. Thanks for the fries. Good night.

Then I lay back in my bed and thought about Ben some more. How I'd get to spend more time with him this week, wondering if he'd ever make an exception to his no dating rule.

A girl could hope, right?

A minute later, my phone buzzed. I scrambled to read it.

Ben: See you tomorrow :)

I may or may not have shrieked.

I had gotten Ben Garcia's number.

14

THE NEXT DAY AT SCHOOL, Ben totally waved to me and said hello in the hallway before first period.

I would've fainted had several girls not immediately locked their laser beam eyes on the one girl who had managed a hello from Ben Garcia.

I mean, he'd only said hi in passing, but we may as well have declared that we were in an exclusive relationship from the looks on a couple of the girls' faces.

Rachel gave me this look, raising one of her brows like she usually did when she said something sassy or made a comeback. "So I take it that the tutoring went well yesterday?"

I nodded, my eyes on Ben's figure in the distance. "We're working on his paper again tonight, actually."

The entire school day, it was a little hard to focus on what the teachers were saying. In cheer, Coach Collins called me out for being half a second behind everyone else.

Oops.

I'd been too busy counting down the hours and then the minutes until Ben and I worked on his paper at Bobby's Cafe after we were each done with practice.

Rachel bopped me on the head with one of her pom-poms. "Come on, girl. Get your head in the game."

Finally, she dropped me off on her way home.

Her stomach growled loud enough for both us to hear.

"Hungry much?" I teased, opening the door to get out.

"Super," she replied, checking her phone. "And my mom just texted that she and my siblings already ate dinner out. So there's no food at home." She pouted.

I glanced at Bobby's behind me. "Come in with me, then. It'll be fun. It's probably busy right now anyway, which means Ben will be busy."

By the time we walked in, Ben was already in his uniform, carrying out plates full of burgers, fries, milkshakes, and a host of other foods.

While he took care of the influx of customers, Rachel and I ordered our own food, going for the usual.

An hour later, the dinner rush had finally died down, but Rachel and I had finished all of our homework.

Her phone buzzed, and she took a look. "I have to get going," she told me, getting up. "This was fun, though."

"Agreed," I replied. "Homework and fries is a pretty snazzy combo."

"#Facts," she said with a wink. Then she leaned in.

"Text me later? Let me know how your hot tutoring session went with… you know who?"

I rolled my eyes but chuckled. "Sure thing. Not that there will be anything to tell," I said, glancing around and making sure Ben was nowhere near earshot.

But he must have been in the back because he was nowhere in sight.

With that, Rachel headed home, and I put away my homework and pushed my empty plate and cup away.

Just as I pulled up Ben's paper on Google docs, he appeared through the double doors. He walked right over. "Sorry. I know it's getting late. Do you have to go yet?" he asked.

I checked the time. It *was* getting kind of late, but Mom had already told me she wouldn't be home until later. "Um, I'm good. And I finished all my homework so… I'm all yours," I finished.

Wow, that sounded forward. Once again, I felt my face flush.

Ben looked away for a second before looking at me again. "Cool. I've just got a few dishes to wash, and I'll be right out."

With that, he carried my dirty dishes away. I called out a thank you.

"Sure thing," he replied, going in through the double doors backwards so he could push them open that way.

Several minutes later, Ben came around with his laptop to my side of the counter and sat down next to me. "All yours," he said.

Not expecting that comment at all, I failed to

respond right away, making the moment kind of awkward.

What was it about me not being able to function when he was around? I had to get it together.

"Okay, so, uh, I was thinking we could work on your conclusion today plus the in-text citations and works cited page," I finally said.

He scooted closer, and I fought back thoughts on whether he needed a better view of what I was showing him on Google Docs or whether he wanted to be a little closer to me.

Google Docs. The answer was Google Docs, especially if I was going to form comprehensible sentences around him.

Over an hour later, we'd made pretty good headway on the rest of his paper. And it was closing time.

Mom let me know she was on her way to pick me up.

I read over Ben's paper one more time, comparing the new version to my notes on the old version and nodding in satisfaction. "I think we're done. You've done as much as you can do. You can turn this into Ms. Wilson tomorrow."

Ben exhaled. "You think so? You think this will get me at least a B?" he asked, sounding kind of nervous.

I turned to him. "For sure. In fact, I'll be surprised if you don't get a B."

He finally cracked a smile. "Thank you," he said. "Seriously."

So I'd given up hours of my limited time here eating

free food and spending time with a boy I had a crazy crush on.

When the other option had been to sit at home alone, eating alone, watching serial killer documentaries on Netflix.

I smiled back. "Happy to help. Seriously."

There was that quick glance towards my mouth again.

Ben shut his laptop, and I did the same.

I got ready to grab my stuff and tell him good night.

But then he said something else. "So how do you know so much about all this stuff?" he asked. "Like history and stuff. When to use citations. The way you explained it made way more sense than in class."

What felt like a heavy stone materialized in my stomach, and I turned so that I was facing the counter again. "Oh, um," I tried, struggling to make up some kind of explanation that didn't require me being utterly vulnerable in front of someone I already found myself caring about.

He was the last person I wanted to break down in front of.

But a big part of me also didn't want to make something up or give a non-answer.

Not to Ben.

I did my best to look at him. "My dad loved history," I said quietly, managing the smallest and quickest of smiles with zero eye contact. "He used to read books about it all the time, read them to me at bedtime even growing up. We watched documentaries together, and he'd explain it all to me in a way that was just...exciting and cool, you know?"

I stopped talking then because my voice threatened to quiver and break, and I was not about to cry. Not here, not tonight.

I couldn't do that.

Exhaling, I chanced another glance at Ben, who'd turned away too.

Finally, he said, "That sounds really cool." He paused. "To have a dad like that."

I bit the inside of my lip, determined to be able to talk about Dad. "He was really cool."

"I'm sorry," he said, his voice hardly audible.

That was it. No questions about what happened or when. Just an "I'm sorry."

I almost sighed in relief.

Before I could say anything, he said something else. "I kinda get what that's like."

I studied his face, the way his eyes focused on his feet, how his mouth turned down a little, and all of a sudden, the entire cafe seemed utterly silent. "I'm sorry," I told him, wishing I could take his hand.

He stood up abruptly, almost like he'd snapped out of a trance. "Um, I should get back to work."

Grabbing his stuff, he said, "Thank you again, really. Let me know when you make it home?" he asked, finally looking at me for half a second.

"Yeah," I nodded.

As I got in Mom's car a few minutes later, I couldn't help but think that I'd never thought I'd have this in common with Ben Garcia.

Rachel, Audrey, and Nora had never mentioned that Ben's dad had died. But in a way, it made sense. No wonder he had to work. No wonder he was the way he was.

And he'd shared that part of himself with me.

And I had done the same.

15

BEN'S next game was less than twenty-four hours away, and I itched to find out what he'd gotten on that paper.

I assumed he would tell me if he'd gotten a B and gotten the go ahead to play in Friday's football game, but he hadn't told me or texted me.

So on Thursday night, just before bed, I worked up the courage and sent him a text.

Scarlett: Hey. So did you find out what you got on that paper?

As I lay in bed trying to fall asleep, my phone buzzed. My hand shot out and grabbed it. I had to slow down and put in my passcode two times before I finally got it right.

Ben: Not yet :/ hopefully tomorrow.

I sighed.

Okay. Tomorrow, we would know. I could wait that long.

Just as I settled into a comfortable position, my

phone buzzed again. This time, I took my time putting in the right passcode.

Ben: Good night.

I immediately smiled, holding back a shriek.

Not what Mom needed to hear at eleven o'clock at night. She'd probably come in with a rolling pin, ready to hit something.

With the cheesiest smile on my face, I texted Ben back.

Scarlett: Good night :)

It took me twice as long to fall asleep just from the giddiness of getting a good night text from Ben.

The next morning, I borrowed a little bit of Mom's undereye concealer. Then I really studied myself in the mirror.

It was me alright, but I also looked different. Because it was game day, I had my uniform top on. My hair was up in a high ponytail, my bow sitting perfectly on top of it. And I'd put on a little extra make up.

If I had seen myself like this a year ago, I never would've believed it.

Dressing up and glamming up for dance was normal, but morphing into a cheerleader? I hadn't seen that one coming. Or my love for it.

Mostly the thrill of it. Much like with dance.

More than ever, I was glad we'd moved to this town and gotten our fresh start. I had no idea if we'd ever go back home. We had family there, on both sides, and I missed them.

But so far, Jefferson had been good for us. Mom was

busy all the time with work but even she seemed better off here.

Tired and kind of overworked but it was also easy to see that she loved what she was doing. That this new house, this new place, had done her a lot of good.

I smiled to myself in the mirror, grabbed my stuff, and left.

As soon as I got to school, I went back to wondering about Ben.

I'd seen him in passing in the morning, but he hadn't seen me. Like the rest of the football team, he had on his football jersey, but I had no idea if that meant he was actually allowed to play that night or not.

And I didn't want to keep asking him about his grade on that paper, as much as I was dying to know.

So I shut my locker and went about my day.

I'd find out sooner or later.

Just before lunch, my phone buzzed.

I pulled it out, expecting a text from Mom or maybe Lily with a cheer update or reminder.

But instead, it was Ben.

Ben: Hey. Where are you?

For a second, I wondered if that text was meant for me. I half expected him to send a "sorry wrong person" text after that, but none came.

I tapped out a response.

Scarlett: My locker. Near the gym.

He didn't reply back after that.

A couple of minutes later, I stood at my locker, my backpack on my shoulders. I hung onto the straps, waiting for Ben to come around the corner.

I assumed he was meeting me. After checking the time on my phone and realizing I was supposed to be headed toward my next class, I bit my lip. Perhaps I needed to text him back and let him know that I was going to be headed towards trig.

But before I could, he came down the hall.

It was impossible to read him. His expression was neutral, his eyes not giving anything away. Like usual.

He came up to me, a stapled and folded essay in his hands. Still, he didn't say anything, and I began to think that maybe he hadn't gotten the grade he needed. That maybe we'd done something wrong, missed something important.

I couldn't take the silence any longer. He needed to look at me and tell me what was going on. "So?" I managed. "Did you get a B?"

That's when he gave a slight shake of his head, biting his lip.

I took the paper from him, immediately unfolding it to see if he had missed getting a B by a few points or what.

A large red A-minus stared back up at me.

What? But…

My head snapped back up.

A wide smile now covered Ben's face. "A minus," he said, beaming.

I laughed, mostly in relief for him. "Wow, this is amazing," I cried, looking back down at the paper. Then I punched him lightly on the shoulder. "You really had me for a second!"

He laughed too. "Sorry. Had to do it."

"It's okay," I replied. I went back to the paper, noticing how few red marks there were on this one compared to the original one. "I guess she loved it."

"Pretty sure those were her exact words, actually," he said, turning so he stood next to me as I flipped through the essay.

I noticed the smiley face beside the conclusion and another one on the Works Cited page.

"I don't think she's ever given me a smiley face on anything," he joked.

I looked up at him and handed him the paper back. "So you get to play tonight?"

He stuck the paper in his backpack. "Yeah, and it's all thanks to you," he said, not looking away for a second while he said it.

Fighting the instinct to look away myself, I grinned. "You're the one who did all the work. I just nudged you in the right direction is all."

Ben scoffed. "I couldn't have done this without you. If it hadn't been for all your help with…everything in that paper, I wouldn't be on the team again. So thank you."

Now I beamed. "You're welcome."

I didn't expect what came next. I blinked and then his arms were around me, his backpack still on the floor in front of him.

Slowly, I put my arms around him too, not believing that Ben was actually giving me a hug.

Then the moment was over.

He pulled his backpack on. "See you at tonight's game?" he asked.

"Kinda have to be," I said with a small laugh. "But yeah."

"Good," he replied, the corner of his mouth turning up into a grin, and once again, I almost floated away with hearts for eyes like in cartoons.

He began to walk away and then I remembered that I had something to give him.

"Wait," I called. "I almost forgot."

I set down my backpack and pulled out a bag of brownies. "These are for you." Inside, there was a note of encouragement. A short and funny poem, really, that I hoped gave the world one of his rare full-on smiles.

"Thanks," he said. "These won't kill me, will they?"

That made us both laugh. I shook my head. "I don't think so." I teased. "But you've got your epipen, right?"

There was that full-on smile I loved. "Just as long as you don't tackle me again."

16

THAT NIGHT AT THE GAME, Ben seemed different.

Good different.

Carried himself different.

Held his head high and his eyes just seemed…happier.

When the announcer called out his name, I landed a perfect round-off on the sidelines. Then I raised my pom-poms and yelled for him, along with everyone else.

Usually, he didn't do much when his name was called. Some of the guys did a funny dance or they waved.

Tonight, Ben turned toward the sidelines where the cheerleaders stood at the ready.

His gaze stopped on me, and I froze, my wide smile faltering.

He gave me a grin, then he winked before turning back to his coach.

Rachel nudged me so hard I about fell right over.

"Oh my gosh!" she screamed. "Did I just see what I thought I saw?"

I turned to her, in disbelief myself. "I don't know," I said. "Did you?"

She screamed, and I found myself screaming along with her.

Lily gave us this look like, "Get it together," so we stopped and got back in our spots.

The game was about to start.

Rachel leaned toward me. "I called it! I swear I did. Ask Audrey and Nora later."

She looked like she had just won the lottery.

"He's just happy he's playing tonight," I fired back. But I couldn't help but keep smiling a cheddar-level cheesy smile.

"Oh, he's happy, alright," Rachel replied. "Happy a certain someone moved to Jefferson. I have never seen Benjamin Garcia give any girl that kind of attention."

I glanced at Ben, the butterflies in my stomach feeling more like helicopters.

Was she right?

I wasn't gonna lie. A big part of me wanted her to be right, wanted Ben to *like me* like me.

But I also didn't want to get my hopes up.

Because until he said or did otherwise, we were just becoming friends and nothing more.

The first thing I'd found out about him was that he didn't date.

Never had.

What would make him change his mind now?

I was just your average girl, the new girl.

And I needed to keep this crush under control.

I turned my attention to the game that was now starting.

Before long, Ben had scored an incredible touchdown, catching an impossible pass and diving into the end zone.

The crowd went wild, and so did we.

The girls threw me into the air.

It wasn't long before Ben helped score another touchdown.

And in the second half, another one.

When the boys finally came off the field, the coach patted Ben on the shoulder and gave him the winning ball.

Then several players came up behind the coach with a giant cooler of Gatorade, dumping the entire thing on his head.

Ben leaped out of the way just in time.

Meanwhile, I followed Rachel onto the field.

I felt more exhausted than ever. It had been a long game, but a good game, and I couldn't wait to get out of there, grab something to eat and crash into bed.

Someone's hand touched my shoulder.

It was Ben.

"You killed it out there tonight," I told him.

"Thank you," he said. "But I would've been sitting on the bench the entire time if it hadn't been for you. So here."

He handed me the game ball.

Our fingers touched for a second. His strong hands dwarfed mine.

"Are you sure?" I asked. "I mean, this is special. You should keep it."

He shook his head. "I want you to have it."

I didn't know what to say after that, but I was careful not to let me eyes turn into hearts in front of him. Tried to keep my smile to more of a swiss-level type cheese instead of full-on cheddar.

He smiled. "Anyway, it can serve as a reminder," he said.

"What do you mean?" I asked.

"Yeah," he went on. "A reminder of the time I almost died because of you."

I almost died laughing.

"And then how you saved my butt in history after that to make up for it," he said. "I mean, if you think about it, if it hadn't been for those death cookies, I might not have gotten this ball anyway."

"Well," I replied. "When you put it that way…"

He smiled. Took another step closer.

His eyes locked on mine, and all of a sudden, I forgot how to breathe properly.

Was it me or did he want to…

A loud and high-pitched voice jarred us back to Earth. "Excuse me, Benjamin Garcia?"

We both turned to find a very skinny girl with a large camera standing about two feet away.

How long had she been there?

She held up her camera? "Can I get a picture for the school paper, please?" she asked, sounding like she might hyperventilate.

I could relate…

Ben nodded. "Uh, yeah, sure."

Just like that, he put his arm around me, without standing too close.

Girl with Camera glanced between me and Ben for a second, and I realized she meant just a photo of Ben. But she gave a slight shrug and snapped a photo, the flash making my head spin.

"Thanks!" she chirped before running off.

I turned back to Ben, but the moment was long over.

"See you at Ryan's party later?" he asked.

Not sure what party he was talking about but making a mental note to ask Rachel, I held onto the football. "Definitely."

Ben opened his mouth like he might say something, but all that came out was, "Sounds good."

Then he was off, a couple of the guys from the team practically engulfing him and clapping him on the back.

I stood there, wondering what Ben had been about to say but mostly ecstatic about said party.

17

AS I WALKED into school a week later, I double-checked my gym bag, making sure I had my entire cheer uniform.

We had a big pep rally later, and I could not afford to forget a single thing.

Bow, top, skirt. Shoes.

Socks… socks?

Oh, I had them on.

I bumped into someone at the doors. "Sorry," I called quickly before rushing in.

For a second, I thought back to Mom. She'd been acting a little weird all morning.

I made a mental note to send her a quick text when I got to first period. Maybe she was having a tough day. It had been a while since I'd had one of those, but sometimes they just hit. I knew them well.

My phone buzzed.

It was Lily, reminding us to get to the pep rally no

less than 30 minutes early so we could practice our routine. She and Coach Collins expected nothing short of perfection, and I did not want to be the one person who flubbed a stunt or forgot a move.

Not after the endless hours of cheer practice, not stopping until we had absolutely nailed every single move.

I yawned as I arrived at my locker.

Plus I had a huge math test later. I'd been up late working on the study guide, trying to figure out trig problems that made me want to tear the whole thing in half.

I wondered briefly if Ben was good at math…

It would be fun to be tutored by him.

I shook my head, remembering that I was supposed to be grabbing books and dashing off to first period.

As if on cue, the warning bell went off.

I really needed to get to class.

After running most of the way there, I made it just in time.

Ms. Collins shut the door behind me. "Good morning, Scarlett. I'm glad you could join us today."

A few kids snickered, and I fought back an eyeroll. My head kind of hurt. I was not in the mood.

After making it through Human A&P, I dragged myself through another several classes. After lunch, I had math. But today it was going to be cut short due to the big pep rally at the end of the day.

It was in the middle of the test that it hit me.

Why Mom had seemed off this morning.

What today was.

I realized in the middle of my math test that I'd forgotten to name and date my paper.

Mrs. Arnold always wrote it on the whiteboard so I glanced up because I could hardly remember what day of the week it was.

October twenty-third.

I blinked, making sure I'd read that right.

I had.

My pencil fell from my hand, and the room spun around me.

It felt difficult to breathe.

Had I really forgotten the anniversary of Dad's passing?

I stared down at my desk in complete disbelief.

After that, I found my legs moving, carrying me toward the door.

"Scarlett? Where are you going?" I heard the teacher say. "We're in the middle of a test."

I hardly stopped, pulling open the door with such force that it flew back and hit the wall behind it.

But I was already gone.

That's when my brain caught up.

Where was I going?

I had no idea.

I just knew I had to get out of there, get away, think.

Be alone for a few minutes. Close my eyes, and…

The tears spilled down my cheeks as I ran into the girls' bathroom down the hall. I walked into the farthest stall, locked it, and pulled down the toilet cover so I could sit.

My head went to my lap, my hands over my face as I tried to contain the semi truck full of emotions that had hit me.

It wasn't long before Steph, one of the girls from cheer, came in, asking if I was okay and saying that Mrs. Arnold was worried about me.

Something about going back to finish my test.

"Um," I tried, using every ounce of energy to make my voice sound normal. "Tell her I don't feel well. I'm gonna go to the nurse's office."

I called out to her before I heard her steps fade away. "Steph? Can you bring me my stuff, please?"

"Sure thing," she said, and she was off, the sound of the door closing echoing throughout the stalls.

I went back to crying, trying to get as much of the hurt and pain out as possible before she was back.

There was guilt for forgetting about Dad on today of all days. Guilt for not remembering and giving mom a reassuring hug before work.

I'd hardly said goodbye that morning before jumping out of the car.

The tears came harder at the thought of her crying at work, thinking that I didn't care. That I cared more about stupid cheer, about this pep rally today.

Then the memories began playing in my head.

The day I came home from school, and as soon as I'd walked in the door, I knew something had gone terribly wrong.

My mom's face crumpling the second she saw me. My grandmother, wrapping her arms around her and then beckoning to me.

The sound of the door shutting closed again had me holding my breath so Steph wouldn't hear me crying. I pulled a giant wad of toilet paper from the roll and wiped my nose.

A familiar but unexpected voice reached me. "Scarlett, what's wrong?" It was Rachel.

Her white sneakers were just on the other side of the stall.

I shook my head. "Nothing," I managed.

"It's not nothing," she said. Her voice came out soft, like she was afraid I might break.

Trouble was, I already had.

After a moment, she added, "Will you open the door, please?"

I stared up at the ceiling. That was actually the last thing I wanted to do. Have her look at me like this. Have to tell her why I looked like this.

"Please, Scarlett? The teacher said I had to come get her if you didn't," Rachel said.

The way she said it, I could tell she wasn't lying and it killed her to have to make me open the door.

Slowly, I stood up and looked at the lock.

My fingers went to it and paused before finally sliding it open.

I stepped out, my gaze on the floor.

Rachel immediately hugged me. "Oh, Scarlett. What happened?"

That only made me start crying again. The fact that I could tell she cared plus the thought of explaining.

I cried for several minutes, letting Rachel hold me while my shoulders racked and the sound of my sobs filled the bathroom.

She rubbed my back and said nothing.

Finally, because I knew class would be ending soon and I didn't want a bunch of animated girls walking into find me crying my eyes out, I took a step back.

Still refusing to meet her eyes, I looked down at my hands instead. "Today," I sniffed, "is the anniversary of my dad's death, and…I forgot." My mouth turned down, and fresh tears filled my eyes.

Rachel took my hands. "Come here." She hugged me again. "Don't let this mean what you're making it mean, okay? You don't love him any less," she said. Then she added, "Or your mom."

All I did was cry some more.

"Promise me," she said, holding my face in her hands. "We've only been friends for a couple of months, but I know you, Scarlett Moore. Promise me you won't beat yourself up over this. No more, okay?"

I shut my eyes, fighting back the painful frog in my throat. I managed to nod a couple of times.

She handed me several paper towels. I wiped away the tears as best as I could and my nose again. Then Rachel grabbed more paper towels and dabbed at my eyes. She grimaced a little.

"Do I look like a rabid raccoon?" I asked.

She gave me a brief smile. "Maybe not rabid, but we will need to re-do your make up." She paused. "Unless you'd rather go home? Coach, everybody, would understand."

Crap.

The pep rally.

I shut my eyes again. Had I remembered what today was I probably wouldn't be in this mess. I ached to go home and get into bed, make Mom join me, but the entire squad was counting on me.

Making them tweak the routine now... I would hate myself for doing that to them.

I opened my eyes. "It's okay. Just help me re-do my make up, okay?" I asked.

"Are you sure?" Rachel asked, studying me closely. "I promise you it's okay to change your mind and decide you don't want to be here right now."

She was right. I definitely didn't want to be there. I didn't want to walk back to class and have everyone see how much I'd been crying.

But I had to.

The mirror a few feet away showed me how pink and puffy my eyes were.

Rachel let go of my hands. "I'm gonna go let the teacher know you're okay. And I'm gonna grab my make-up bag. I'll be right back, okay? By the time we're done here, it'll be time for us to head to the gym anyway."

I nodded. "Thanks."

While she did that, I went over to the sink and dabbed my eyes with wet paper towels, hoping that helped with the puffiness.

Then I pulled out my phone and opened up my texts to Mom.

Scarlett: <3 Love you, Mom. More than ever.

I wanted to say more, let her know that I remembered what today was, but I didn't know how to word it. She would know.

As soon as I saw her later, she would know.

Not even a minute later, she texted me back.

Mom: <3 Love you, sweetheart. More than you'll ever know.

Rachel came back in. "Mrs. Arnold said it was okay, that you can finish your test tomorrow if you're up for it."

I exhaled. "Thank goodness." Mrs. Arnold was the type of teacher that could be kind of severe at times, but I was so glad she had decided to let me finish the test despite just running out of class.

Then Rachel set her make up bag on the counter. She began by pulling out a make up remover wipe. "Okay, let's do this."

By the time she was done, I looked ten times better than when I'd done my own make up. The mirror reflected a small smile on my face, the kind that struggled to reach my eyes. "Wow," I said. "You're gonna have to teach me how to do this look."

She zipped up her make up bag with a flourish. "Anytime, chica." She winked at me in the mirror. "I've got your back. Never forget it."

My smile grew a little wider. "Right back at ya."

She gave me a grin before checking her phone. "Okay, if we're not in the gym in two minutes, Coach is gonna freak." But then she stopped. "Are you sure you're good?"

I blew out a breath. My gut told me no, but my head said I needed to go do this. The team was counting on me. "I'm good."

I followed Rachel to the gym, hoping that I could focus long enough to get through the pep rally.

18

AS SOON AS I stepped onto the gym floor, in front of a school full of plastic bleachers, I regretted not going home.

I felt bile rise up in my throat, and I fought to keep it down.

The tears were back, making my vision blurry, but I held on to my pom-poms anyway.

Every time the football coach announced one of his players' names, I raised my pom-poms in the air and did my best to cheer.

Finally, he encouraged everyone to come out to our home games to support the school. Said something about the cheerleaders and what a great job we'd been doing. I raised my pom-poms again and did my best to smile.

Then I heard Coach Collins's voice come on the mic. I knew what this meant. It was time for our routine, the one that was supposed to wow everyone, get them pumped up, and eventually win us several competitions.

I stepped onto the large blue mats along with the rest of the squad. For some reason, my legs felt kind of numb and the noise from the crowd in the bleachers sounded too loud and yet distant at the same time.

Taking a deep breath, I glanced at Rachel, who shot me a look of concern. But before she could do anything else, the gym grew quiet. I automatically turned my gaze down, waiting for the music to begin.

The song began, and with it, a thousand thoughts flashed through my head. Thoughts about Mom and Dad. Thoughts of this day four years ago.

I tried to keep up, but I could tell I was just a tad behind the rest of the squad.

Then I turned in left instead of right, and the tears threatened to spill over again. Frustration, grief, and everything in between.

I had to do this. Just another couple of minutes.

But I messed up again, and this time, I wasn't sure I could keep the tears at bay.

I knew this routine, so why couldn't I remember what to do?

We got ready for the first of several stunts. I joined Rachel and the other girls who usually threw me up into the air.

"Come on, Scarlett," I heard Rachel say. "You can do this."

Could I? I doubted everything I had become, especially since coming to Jefferson.

I put my foot in Rachel's hands, held onto the

shoulders to either side of me, and then the girls launched me up.

This wasn't like any other time I'd gone up, though. My sense of balance was way off. I struggled to keep my body firm and straight even though I'd done it dozens of times before today.

My foot slipped abruptly from one of the girls' hands, and I fell. Fear and adrenaline surged through me, and I anticipated the pain of some part of me hitting the blue mat. But I didn't.

Several strong arms caught me and let me hit the mat gently. Before I could even say thank you, the girls were off. The routine was still underway, and there I was, still partially on the ground.

There was Coach Collins, urging me to get up and move. My knees felt stuck to the ground, though.

My gaze turned to the bleachers. Several eyes found me, confused expressions. Whispers. Then pointing.

It was just like the first day I'd gone back to school after Dad had died.

My mind flashed back to me walking down the hallway. No one had come up and said hello. Everyone had just stared and whispered like I wasn't right there. Only Anne had come over and made sure I was okay.

I had to get out of there.

If I stayed in that gym one more second…

I pushed off my knees and stood then ran toward the double doors. Luckily, they weren't too far. I lunged through them open and kept running until I made it to my locker. I twisted the dial, wanting to grab my stuff so I could just leave somehow.

The locker didn't open. I blew out a breath and tried again.

Maybe I could call Mom, ask her to pick me up.

No, Mom was at work. In meetings and stuff. I'd wait in the nurse's office. The school day was almost over. Rachel could give me a ride home. Then I wouldn't have to ride the bus for half an hour before it reached my stop.

Yeah, that worked.

Anything but going back to the gym or any kind of classroom.

The locker opened, and I grabbed my stuff. Grabbed my phone and my book bag.

My gym bag was still in the girls' locker room in the gym, but that was the least of my worries.

I made my way down the hallway toward the school nurse.

It was near the front office, which meant I had to go through the catwalk to get to the main building.

On the left there was the parking lot and the exit, but on the right there was a garden in between the two buildings. It was the same little garden and bench I walked past every day.

I made my way over to it, thankful for the solitude.

In a few minutes, I could text Rachel asking her for a ride home. But until then, I wanted to just sit and not think about anything.

Definitely not about the humiliation I'd have to endure tomorrow after showing my face. About potentially getting kicked off the squad by Mrs. Collins for running off in the middle of a routine. About the rest of the squad hating me.

I imagined them trying to finish the rest of the routine without me, none of it looking right or going right.

I hadn't just embarrassed myself. I'd embarrassed them.

Great.

I exhaled. So much for having a great start at Jefferson. Time to talk to Mom about moving again.

Not.

This kind of worry was the last thing she needed, especially today.

All I wanted was to go home and rest my head in her lap like I did when I was little and any time I had a bad day.

A few tears ran down my cheeks. I wiped them away, not wanting to ugly cry for the second time in less than a couple of hours.

Today had been the definition of a bad day.

I exhaled and looked around at the garden. A few rose bushes still had some roses on them, but mostly lay bare.

The ground was covered in small pebbles. I reached down and picked one up. Holding it in my hand, feeling the smooth surface, made me feel a little better.

I got a better look at the bench too.

It was a memorial bench.

Someone had put it here twelve years ago in honor of someone named Jonathan and Maggie Stuart. For being true heroes of the community.

I wondered who they'd been, what they'd been like.

As I turned to face the parking lot, I realized that one day, Dad would be dead twelve years. So far it had only been four. But one day it would be five, six, ten, twelve.

Twenty.

I'd go to college and he wouldn't be there to wish me luck and remind me that I could call him day or night for homework help.

One day I'd walk down the aisle, but only Mom would be at my side.

There was so much he'd miss.

A single tear ran down my cheek, and I wiped it away too.

There had been a lot of really hard days in the last four years. Today was one of them.

Deciding to come here? Packing? So hard.

But I also couldn't remember the last time Mom and I had actually been pretty happy since losing Dad.

But even so, the hard days followed us everywhere.

I wiped another tear away.

The sound of the doors opening made me look in that direction.

I expected a wave of students to come pouring out, ready to head home, but only one did.

Ben.

His gaze found me. I looked away.

"Hey," he said, walking over. "Rachel's been looking for you. Said you weren't replying to her texts."

Oops. I'd thrown my phone in my backpack and hadn't give it a thought since.

"Guess I forgot to check it," I replied softly.

He stood in front of me and gestured to the bench. "May I?" he asked.

I nodded.

"Are you okay?" he asked, taking a seat beside me.

Ugh. I hated that question, especially right now.

How was I supposed to answer it?

"I will be," I tried.

More silence.

"Is there anything I can do?" he asked.

I blinked, still not wanting to look up at Ben because the way he had to be looking at me right now, it was the kind of thing that made a girl fall in love with a boy, and I wasn't sure I could handle it.

I shook my head. "I just want to go home."

Right. I needed to text Rachel. Without even thinking about it, I did look up at him. His emerald green eyes stared back at me. But instead of their usual hardness, they seemed soft. "Um, can you text Rachel for me? Tell her I said can she give me a ride home?"

"Yeah," he replied, pulling his phone from his back pocket. He tapped out a quick text. In the meantime, students began pouring out of the building we'd come out of.

I did my best to just keep my gaze on the ground.

"Rachel says she's supposed to go straight home to take care of her brothers, but she will help you figure something out," Ben read from his phone.

I sighed. "Okay. I'll just meet up with her in a minute," I said, standing up. I needed to get going anyway.

Maybe it would be best just to take the bus home as usual.

I'd forgotten that Rachel had mentioned having to babysit this afternoon.

"Wait," Ben said. "I don't mind taking you home."

I stopped. "I couldn't ask you to do that. You've got practice."

He checked his phone. Not for another thirty minutes. If we go now…" His voice trailed off as he glanced at the parking lot. If we hurried, we could be the first ones out and avoid the usual afternoon traffic jam.

Before I could think too much about it, I said, "Okay."

He gave me a small smile and pulled out his keys from his jeans pocket. "Come on."

We made our way to the student parking lot in record time. He led me to an older forest green Jeep, opening the passenger door for me.

"Thanks," I said, hopping in.

He came around, texting someone before turning on the car. "Letting Coach know I might be a few minutes late."

"Won't you get in trouble?" I asked.

Ben shrugged. "Worst that can happen is he'll give me extra drills."

"Thank you," I replied.

He met my gaze for a second, his hand still on the keys in the ignition. "Glad I could help."

Ben put the Jeep in reverse and pulled out of the school. I pointed right. "My house is that way."

I texted him my address, and he turned on his GPS then some music. He kept it down low, which was perfect.

For the first time that day, I finally felt myself relax a little. My shoulders slumped, and I let myself rest back in the seat.

Ben glanced my way a couple of times but kept his eyes on the road.

I closed mine, relieved that I was finally headed home. In just a few minutes, I would be under the covers of my bed. Nothing could hurt me there.

Ben's voice broke the silence between us. "It's hard losing your dad. I get it."

I looked at him, not sure how much I could talk about this. If I even wanted to.

His face had hardened, and he looked straight ahead. Something told me it had taken a lot for him to say those few words.

Didn't he deserve the same?

I exhaled. "Today was four years since it happened."

He turned down the music. Stayed silent a little while longer then replied, "I think I was seven? It's hard to remember him."

Seven? So he'd gone closer to ten years without his dad.

I couldn't even imagine growing older and finding it more and more difficult to remember my dad. Forgetting what his face looked like. What his voice sounded like.

It's the reason the photos and videos we had of him

were precious to us. They were all we had left of him. That and the memories, and memories faded.

"Does it ever get easier?" I asked.

Ben shrugged. "I don't think so."

Ben kept driving, and I glanced at him. Saw his hand on the console between us. I wanted to reach over and take it, but I was too chicken to do it.

What if I ruined the moment? Maybe he was just being nice. A good friend.

Finally, he pulled into my driveway and came to a stop.

"Thank you," I said. "Really."

He gave me a nod. "Any time."

Grabbing my backpack, I went to open the door. But Ben was already out of his Jeep and halfway around.

He opened my door for me, making me smile for the first time all day.

"Thanks," I said. Not knowing what else to do, I took a couple of steps toward the front door. "See you at school tomorrow?"

"Yeah," Ben said.

"Okay," I replied softly, turning to go.

"Scarlett?" he said.

I stopped. Turned.

He didn't say anything, though. Instead, he closed the gap between us and wrapped his arms around me.

Setting my book bag down on the driveway, I hugged him back too.

Breathed him in. Closed my eyes. Found relief.

His hug was long and warm and perfect.

It was what I didn't even know I needed.

I had to stand on my toes to reach him, and I loved that. Loved his firm chest and broad shoulders. It felt like nothing could hurt me so long as Benjamin Garcia held me.

He pulled away, and an instant later, I ached for his touch again.

Before I could say anything or even think of what I could say, he gave me a kind smile and was off. He gave me a small wave as he pulled of out my driveway. I waved back and went inside, still kind of light-headed from that amazing hug.

I locked the front door behind me and headed to my room, my bed calling to me.

But the sight of my mom's large purse on the counter had me stopping in my tracks.

I peeked into the garage, and sure enough, her car was there.

How long had she been home? She hadn't been home earlier than seven o'clock in weeks.

I went off in search of her, making my way down the hallway and to her room.

After a couple of soft knocks, I went in.

Sure enough, she was there, curled up in bed. She lifted her head groggily from her pillow. I could tell she'd been crying. "Scarlett?" Her voice sounded a little confused. She had to have been sleeping for a while.

"Mom," I said, rushing over. I gave her a giant hug. "I'm sorry I didn't remember this morning." The tears came back so quickly.

She made room for me, and I crawled into bed right

alongside her. "Oh, honey," she said, putting her arm around me. "It's okay."

I shook my head. It totally wasn't.

She hugged me tight, kissing me on the head. "How was school?" she asked.

"Terrible," I replied. I told her about the pep rally. She told me about skipping an important meeting to come home and just sleep and forget what today was.

I began to fall asleep myself, just hearing her talk. The sound of her voice calmed me.

After a few minutes, she began to get out of bed. "How about I cook us some real food?" she asked, sounding not quite so sad anymore.

"Are you sure?" I asked, my eyes already closed.

"Yeah," she whispered. "It'll be ready by the time you're awake. It'll be good for me to get up and move."

That was the last thing I heard before I finally gave in and let sleep take over.

19

THE NEXT MORNING, I got to first period early, hoping to catch Mrs. Collins so I could apologize for letting the squad down.

Her classroom was completely empty, but I knocked a couple of times anyway before walking in.

She looked up from her desk, and I gave her a tight-lipped smile, not sure how upset she was going to be or what kind of punishment she'd dish out.

"Scarlett," she said, her face blank. "Good morning."

"Good morning," I replied, walking over to her. Eyes down, I began. "I just wanted to come in and say sorry about the pep rally yesterday. I know I messed up the whole thing and after all of our hard work…"

Rachel had texted me last night, asking if I was okay. And then I had asked her about what had gone down after I'd run away.

Two words.

Not good.

The rest of the routine had pretty much fallen apart after I'd left, and it was all my fault.

Mrs. Collins sighed. "Thank you for coming in and saying that. I know it can't be easy." She stood up and came around her desk. "The truth is Rachel told me what was going on yesterday."

Oh.

I had been wondering if I was gonna have to tell her why I'd gotten so upset and freaked out.

Mrs. Collins gave me a sympathetic look. "I don't blame you, Scarlett. Not at all. I can't imagine what you were going through yesterday."

"Thank you," I managed. I'd decided that morning that I'd cried enough yesterday and there would be no more tears today, but this conversation was threatening to ruin that.

She touched my shoulder. "I'm glad to see you're doing better today," she said with a smile. "Besides, there will always be another pep rally, another competition, another opportunity to do better. No one's perfect all the time."

I smiled. "You make a good point."

"Also," she went on." I want you to know that you can come to me for anything, tell me anything. Okay?"

I nodded, relief flooding my system. "That means a lot."

Several students began filing in so I took my seat.

That had gone a lot better than I'd expected.

I felt better too.

Yesterday had been pretty sucky. A nap, a good

meal, a fun movie, and ten hours of sleep had worked wonders.

And that legendary hug from Ben hadn't been too shabby either. I'd even dreamed about it, not that I would ever admit that out loud.

Nope, the knowledge of that hug would remain for me and me only.

I couldn't wait to see Ben again.

The boys had another game tonight, which meant watching him play and then hanging out after.

It made me nervous to think about how I was supposed to act around him. We were friends, but we'd shared some personal things. We'd spent time together working on that paper.

And did I mention the hug he'd given me?

Was I crazy to think that maybe he liked me?

It was so hard to tell with Ben.

I hadn't seen him act like that with any other girl since I'd arrived at Jefferson, and neither had Rachel. He hardly looked at a girl, much less made physical contact.

But then again, he didn't date.

So I didn't want to get my hopes up or misinterpret things.

I wasn't sure I could take any heartbreak.

Then again, what if he had changed his mind?

A girl could dream, right?

It wasn't outside the realm of possibility…

I wanted to find out. If things kept going the way they were going…

I decided to start by at least thanking him for everything he'd done for me yesterday.

Maybe that would give me a good feel for where we stood.

The thought of going up to Ben later and possibly getting friend zoned had me more scared than getting thrown up into the air.

But what if Ben was willing to break his own no-dating rule?

I had to find out.

20

AFTER A TOUGH LOSS, most of the cheer squad and football team headed to Bobby's.

That was the thing about the food there. Burgers and fries made victory all the more sweet.

But there also wasn't a lot that a good milkshake couldn't fix.

I spotted a couple of empty seats next to Ben and Aaron, shooting a glance at Rachel.

She led me over there.

Aaron saw us coming and moved down a couple of seats so Rachel and I could sit in between him and Ben.

I smiled at Ben as I sat down, and he did the same.

"Hey," I said. "Good game tonight."

"Thanks," he replied. "Wasn't our best, but…"

"You did your best, though," I said, shivering a little. "And that's what matters."

"Glad you think so," he replied. "Coach didn't, so we have extra practices this weekend."

"Yeah," Aaron chimed in. "At six o'clock in the morning."

Ben shut his eyes like he already wasn't looking forward to being up that early. He seemed tired.

A lot of the time, he sported dark circles under his eyes, and tonight was no exception.

He looked a little bit like a deflated balloon.

I tried to say something to perk him up, wishing I could help him feel better the way he'd done for me the day before. "Maybe you can take a nap after practice is over."

He grinned, but still seemed sleepy. "Sure. If by nap, you mean come and work an eight-hour shift here."

I grimaced for his sake. "And I thought I had it bad with laundry day tomorrow."

The waitress came over and took our order. I asked for a large chocolate shake plus a burger and fries.

Ben got the same, minus the shake.

Then we went back to silence.

I opened my mouth, not wanting to think too much before what I was about to say. "Listen, I just wanted to thank you—"

Just then, a couple more football players walked in. Everyone erupted in cheers. They laughed about something.

Ben gave a, "What?" but it was almost impossible to hear him.

Great.

I shook my head. Maybe later.

"Let's go outside," Ben tried, nodding toward the exit and standing up.

I followed him, glancing back at Rachel who winked.

There was a bench farther down the shopping center, in front of a store that was closed for the night. Ben led me there and sat down.

I did the same, shivering a little and wishing I'd thought to grab my jacket.

Ben took off his letterman jacket. "Here," he said, placing it around my shoulders.

"Are you sure?" I asked, not believing I was now wearing his still warm varsity jacket.

"Yeah," he replied. "I mean, I'd be cold too if I was wearing that cheer uniform."

I looked down at my skirt and bare legs. The top left my arms bare too. "You make a good point." Meanwhile, Ben had changed out of his football uniform and into jeans and a nice black shirt along with his jacket.

We kinda laughed and then got quiet.

Right. I had been about to say something.

I did my best to make eye contact instead of staring around awkwardly while I talked. "Anyway, um, I just wanted to say thank you for giving me a ride home yesterday, and…just being a really good friend."

Why did that sound a lot more dorky coming out of my mouth than I had rehearsed in my head?

It's like I was missing the totally cool and confident version of me, the one who knew when to flip her hair. Instead, there was only the actual me, who was just trying not to shiver from the cool breeze or stumble over her words.

Ben met my eyes, his green ones soft again. "It was no problem. I'm glad you're better today."

I nodded. "Doing cheer, the friday night games, it helps."

"Yeah," he replied. "I like staying busy too."

"Busy is good," I said.

Busy is good??

I wanted to take off his jacket and cover my whole head with it.

"You know what?" he asked.

Keep it cool, keep it cool. "What?" I replied.

"So…" He glanced away. "I'm really glad you moved here. And that you joined cheer. And that you almost killed me," he went on, laughing. "Otherwise, I would be flunking social studies and I'd be off the team and we wouldn't be hanging out."

It took me a second to make sure he'd really just said that. My body threatened to just float away.

Say something, say something! "I…I am really glad that I moved here too."

Was it me, or had he leaned in a little.

One thing was for sure. He hadn't been sitting this close just a few minutes earlier. Had he?

His face, his mouth, was right there.

If I leaned forward just a little…

The way he looked at me, it was like he was trying to say something with his eyes that he couldn't bring himself to say out loud.

I knew the feeling.

I waited for him to continue leaning, come closer, and do what I so wanted him to do.

His eyes shifted to hesitation, though, and I wondered if he was about to pull away.

A thought popped into my head.

Did I dare?

"Ben?" I heard myself say. My voice was soft and unsure, but his eyes flashed, the hesitation gone.

My eyes closed on their own as I leaned toward him and let my mouth touch his.

Just like that, I was kissing him.

It was the craziest thing I'd ever done, and I loved it.

After a second, Ben kissed me back too, slowly at first and then…not.

We pulled away. I sat back, my chest rising and falling.

A minute ago, I'd gone in sure of myself, but now I wasn't sure how I felt.

Nervous, maybe?

Should I have kissed Ben?

What if this wasn't what he wanted?

I tried to read the expression on his face, but he seemed kind of nervous too.

He didn't look away from me, though. "I kind of have a confession to make" he said.

"What do you mean?" I asked, pulling his jacket closer around me.

"You know how you guys get assigned a football player for the season?" he went on, a small smile creeping onto his face.

"Yeah…" I said, trying to guess what he was about to say next.

"Um, I kind of requested you," he said, kind of embarrassed. He glanced away.

I looked at him, confused. "Rachel told me Coach Collins makes the assignments."

His eyes met mine. "Yeah, but Rachel also kind of hinted one day that maybe Lily helps. And I kind of asked Lily to…assign you to me."

I couldn't help but laugh. Rachel! I should've known.

Ben gave me a sheepish grin, and I smiled back. "You asked Lily to… why would you do that?"

He looked down for a second. "I guess I kinda had a crush on the new girl, and I wanted to get to know you."

That had me smiling. "Really?"

He nodded. "Little did I know… the new girl would almost kill me."

I started laughing, and so did he. "I will never hear the end of that, will I?" I demanded.

"Nope," he replied.

We smiled, and I about pinched myself because this could not be my life.

Ben checked his phone. "We should probably head back? I bet our food is almost ready."

Oh, yeah. Food.

It was the whole reason we'd even gone to Bobby's.

We stood up and headed back inside.

Rachel and Aaron were already eating. My chocolate shake was waiting for me. The entire time I had it, I couldn't help but think that, as delicious as it was, it couldn't compare to kissing Ben.

21

BEN and I texted back and forth over most of the weekend.

He couldn't always talk because of football practice and work, but his good morning and good night texts became everything.

Even though he hadn't actually asked me to be his girlfriend or anything, I liked where things were going.

I liked that we were talking and getting to know each other.

But mostly, I really liked Ben.

He had dreams of college ball, maybe trying for pro, but mostly trying to get a good job so he could help his mom buy a nice house one day. Help his brothers pay for school.

I got the idea that his mom kind of struggled when it came to money, and that's why Ben worked so many hours at Bobby's.

When I told Mom a little bit about it, she said, "Wow, single mom of five boys. Just thinking about that makes me exhausted," she quipped. "Not to mention broke."

I nodded. She had a point.

We had it pretty good. When Dad had passed away, he had at least left behind some money. Dad had always been good at managing their money and making sure money had been set aside in a savings account. So Mom and I had been okay. Not rich, by any means, but Mom had been able to take a couple of months off and properly mourn. But it was only because Dad had been the type of person who always prepared for everything.

I couldn't imagine losing Dad and then Mom also struggling to pay bills.

I'd never met Ben's mom before, but I had a feeling she had to be extraordinary.

And clearly, it was where Ben got it from too.

On Monday morning, Ben walked me to class.

No holding hands or anything like that, but I thought it was great all the same.

One of his brothers came up to us on our way there.

"Hey," his brother said. He flashed a tight-lipped smile at me. "Hi."

"Hi," I replied.

He turned back to Ben, who introduced him. "Scarlett, this is my brother Drake. Drake, Scarlett."

"Nice to meet you," I said, giving him a quick wave and holding on to my books.

"Likewise," he replied quickly, hardly looking at me again. Then he pulled Ben aside.

Unlike Aaron, Drake seemed kind of…withdrawn.

I hated to use the word "mean." I didn't really know him.

But he definitely had this bad boy vibe going on. Messy hair, dark clothes, and a brooding demeanor that would make Severus Snape proud.

In fact, he could've passed for an attractive teen Snape...

I shook my head and stifled a laugh.

I had to tell Rachel, Audrey, and Nora.

No.

No, no, no.

Drake left, and Ben and I resumed walking to class.

On the way there, another guy waved bye to us.

"That's Cade," he said, waving back.

"Cade," I repeated. "Who's older? Cade or Drake? Or Aaron?"

Ben counted on his fingers. "Me, Aaron, Cade, Drake, and then there's Eli. Or as we like to call him: Squirt."

I grinned. "Just so long as you guys don't give me a weird nickname."

"Oh," he replied. "We already have." He paused. "Killer cookie girl."

I laughed. "Oh my gosh." So that name *had* stuck.

Thanks a lot, Rachel...

"Kind of has a nice ring to it," he said, grinning wide.

I shook my head. "I hate you." But I smiled at him.

We said bye at the door to Mrs. Benson's room.

I found my seat. Nora was there, just a couple seats away. "You are in so much trouble," she teased.

Pulling open my binder, I replied, "I've never loved being in trouble more than I do now."

It was like that the rest of the week.

Walking to class together sometimes. Texting. Looking forward to Friday night football games and hanging out together after.

Life was good.

I still missed Dad, and the hole he'd left in our lives still felt large and gaping at times, but overall, I felt happy. Mom seemed happy. Busy but happy. Apparently, there was some guy at the office who had asked her to dinner, but she wasn't sure how she felt about it.

We talked about it one night. I had been about to go to bed, but then she'd come home. I'd barely seen her the entire week so I joined her in the kitchen while she grabbed a bite to eat.

"How do you feel about this guy?" I asked. She hadn't really dated more than once or twice since Dad had died.

She sighed. "I don't know. Sometimes I think I might like him, like I want to give it a try, and sometimes, I think... he's not your dad."

This intense sadness swept over her face when she said that.

I stood up and gave her a hug. "I think when the right person comes along, you'll know. Just make sure you don't close off your heart forever."

She smiled up at me. "How did I get such a wise teenager? And one who hasn't screamed 'I hate you' at me even once?"

I giggled. "No idea."

She went back to eating. "Goodness knows I yelled that every other week at my mom growing up…" she muttered. "Then again, I'm not your grandma."

"You're right about that," I said, grabbing a snack from the fridge.

Grandma could be a little…intense. Even if she did have good intentions.

Good thing she had Grandpa to balance her out.

I turned back to Mom, opening up my Greek yogurt. "So when do you think you'll come to one of the games?"

She grimaced, putting down her fork. "Oh, honey, I am so sorry. This project has gone on longer than I anticipated. But I will make it to one of them. Promise." She paused. "When does the season end?"

I grabbed a spoon. "Soon. Maybe a month."

She nodded. "Got it. If not the next one, then… definitely the next one."

But the way she didn't quite make eye contact when she said it, I wasn't so sure she actually could. I didn't press the issue, though.

I could tell this project and possible promotion at work was important to her, and she deserved to be happy.

I wanted to tell her about Ben, but just as I opened my mouth to do so, Mom's phone went off.

She immediately unlocked it, pushing away her plate. "Uh oh. Important email. I need to make a quick call." She stood up and headed into the living room.

After finishing my yogurt and tossing the spoon into the sink, I peeked into the living room, but Mom was still on the phone. Plus she'd gotten her laptop out and was typing away.

"Are you sure that's how we should word it?" she asked.

I walked up to her and leaned down to give her a kiss good night. She looked up for half a second, mouthed "sorry," and went back to work. I left.

On the way to my room, I couldn't help but think about how much I wanted to tell her about Ben, but it just hadn't felt right. I usually told Mom everything. Crushes, embarrassing moments, epic fails.

She knew about the pep rally and the killer cookies.

But my mood had turned a little sour after our initial conversation. And then work had called her away again.

Just a little longer, I told myself. This project at work? It wouldn't last forever, and then we'd be back to our normal lives where we spent several nights a week watching hilarious movies, eating crazy amounts of food, and doing other fun stuff.

In the meantime, I had cheer, my friends, and Ben.

22

BEN: Hey, want to hang out after practice is over? I'll be working, but if you like free food...

And just like that, my feelings for Ben grew deeper.

Free food? Hang out with Ben?

Exceptional eye candy while I solved trig problems?

I was there.

Scarlett: Count me in :)

I may or may not have walked to class after lunch with the widest grin in human history after that.

Ben had asked me to hang out.

After taking deep breaths and focusing on not flailing, I took a seat next to Rachel. "Hey," I said, a little too loudly.

She gave me this look like she could tell something was off. "What happened to you?"

I folded my lips in to keep from giving a loud SQUEEE. Then I exhaled. "Ben asked me to hang out today."

Rachel blinked and her left brow shot up. "Really?"

I nodded. "Isn't this great?"

"It's awesome," she said. "Sounds like he no longer cares about his no dating rule." She winked at me. "Good for you. New girl sweeping in and snatching up Ben Garcia just like that." She looked me up and down like she'd never really seen me before. "I'm impressed, new girl."

I laughed. "Whatever. You make it sound like I'm something special, but I'm not."

Rachel leaned in close, and her face went all fierce. "Uh, yeah, you are. Don't let anyone tell you different."

I smiled. "I love you," I replied, facing forward. I winked at her. "Tyra Banks."

She laughed at that one.

The bell rang, and the teacher asked for homework.

But first, Rachel turned to me and smiled. "Same, new girl."

After cheer practice, Rachel pulled me aside in the locker room. She looked me up and down again, but this time, I could tell it was an assessment. "Okay, we've got some work to do."

I smiled. "What do you mean?" I checked myself out in the mirror. So my hair was a little messy and my face was still sweaty, but all of that could be easily fixed.

Rachel joined me in front of the mirror. "We've got to touch up the makeup and fix the hair, minimum." She looked at my post-practice leggings and t-shirt. "You didn't bring any other clothes, did you?" she asked, tone completely serious.

"Um," I said, not sure if I should be offended. "No?"

She let out a disappointed sigh. "I guess we'll have to work with this."

Now I laughed. "Okay."

Count on Rachel to turn this into a big deal. "You know we're just hanging out, right? Doing homework? Talking?"

Rachel gave me an unimpressed look. "It's practically a first date. And we're talking about the hottest guy in school, one who has never once dated or had a girlfriend, like ever. Except for maybe in sixth grade." She looked away for a few seconds, like she was trying to remember something. "Maybe Jenny Vasquez? I remember she moved away…" She shook her head a little, regaining focus. "Anyway, this is sooo much more than a first date, if you really think about it."

That definitely got me thinking. Did Rachel have a point?

All of a sudden, I noticed my messy mascara and eyeliner and the two thousand flyaways around my face. "Rachel?" I turned to her, a little bit of panic in my voice. "Transform me."

Fifteen minutes later, my hair was straight and shiny thanks to Rachel's emergency mini hair straightener. My make up was redone and better than ever. I blinked in the mirror, admiring the subtle yet sparkly eyeshadow she'd applied. Not to mention the cat eye eyeliner. "Rachel, you are a magician."

She zipped up her make up bag. "Gracias."

I stared at myself in the mirror, eyes wide. "You know, I wasn't nervous before, but now I think I am."

Rachel stood next to me, looking at my reflection too. "Well, just don't go in looking like that."

23

THANKFULLY, Bobby's was in the middle of a dinner rush when I walked in, so I didn't have too much to worry about.

Ben was nowhere to be seen.

I found my usual spot at the counter up near the front.

Ben came practically running out the double doors to the back, several plates in his hands. He carried three plates up to his right elbow and another in his left hand.

He gave me a quick smile. "Hey," he said, as he dashed past.

I gave him a small wave and began pulling out books and homework.

By the time I was done with that night's homework, the dinner rush had died down and Ben finally sat down next to me. "Sorry," he said. "It's not usually this busy on a Wednesday, plus one of our cooks is out."

"It's okay," I said, shutting my math book. "I'm pretty much done with my assignments, so it's all good."

He smiled. "Does that mean you can help me with mine?" he asked, making me think of the nervous laughter emoji.

"That can be arranged," I replied. "For the right price."

The bell from the kitchen rang, and he stood up. "Large order of fries. Coming right up."

I laughed and watched him go.

A cute boy who brought me free fries. It just didn't get better than this.

Several minutes later, the restaurant just about emptied out. Ben brought over the promised order of fries, and we dug in.

"I've got a couple of burgers coming out in a minute too," he said, "but I couldn't wait anymore. I'm starving."

"Me too," I said, dipping a French fry into Bobby's sauce then popping it into my mouth.

We spent the better part of the next hour doing his homework and eating a late dinner.

When it came to math, he definitely got the hang of it faster than me and finished the homework in almost half the time it took me.

I looked through them, comparing his answers to mine. "How can you do these that fast? I mess up if I don't go at a snail's pace."

He shrugged and picked up the rest of his burger. "It's an acquired skill, especially when the more time you spend on homework, the less sleep you get."

The closer it got to nine o'clock, the more I dreaded going home. This time, Mom was out of town through

Saturday so I was going home to an empty house and staying in one for a few days.

I could've asked Rachel, Audrey, or Nora if I could stay with them, but the thought of not sleeping in a familiar place each night sounded slightly worse, even if it was with friends.

My phone buzzed. I checked it. "My Uber's almost here," I said.

I grabbed my stuff, and Ben walked me out.

"Thank you for dinner," I said. "Again."

"Thanks for hanging out," he replied. "Even if it is kind of lame that I have to work."

I looked up at him. "I just think it's cool that 'Bobby' lets you do homework and hang out while it's slow."

That made him laugh. "Yeah, Bobby is pretty cool, I gotta admit."

Seeing him laugh only made me smile wider. I loved his laugh, and I loved that I got to hear it more and more often lately.

Ben slipped his hand around mine. "Text me when you get home?" he asked quietly.

"Yeah," I said. "I will."

For a second, I thought he was going to lean down and kiss me, but he didn't. Instead, he wrapped his arms around me.

As much as I would've preferred a kiss from him, settling for a hug wasn't half bad.

On my way home, my phone buzzed. I expected it to be Mom, asking what I was doing or Rachel asking how my "date" with Ben had gone.

But it wasn't either of them.

Ben: By the way, you looked beautiful tonight.

After that, I pretty much floated from my Uber to my front door.

Thank you, Rachel.

24

OUR NEXT COUPLE of games were away, which meant hopping onto a bus to play at a school a good hour or more from town.

I was one of the first people on the bus so I found a seat near the back, leaned my head against the window, and closed my eyes.

I'd been up way too late watching Netflix before I'd remembered that I had a science test in first period.

So instead of heading to bed at midnight, I had groaned out loud and pulled the study guide from my backpack to study.

And it happened to be one of those units where there were like a dozen human muscles to memorize. So I was ready for a nap.

Even though someone sat down next to me, I kept my eyes closed. "Wake me up when we get there, okay, Rach?" I mumbled.

"Okay," I heard from someone who was definitely not Rachel.

I sat up so fast, wiping the sleep from my eyes.

Ben started laughing so hard. "I'm sorry," he said, still laughing. "I didn't mean to scare you."

I stared at him, still kind of startled. Blinked several times. "Well, I am no longer sleepy. So, thank you for that."

I couldn't help it, though. I smiled, and our eyes met.

Rachel walked past, giving me a wave and a wink.

"Is it okay if I sit with you?" Ben asked, the ghost of a smile still present on his handsome face.

"Yeah," I said, nodding. "Of course."

Always.

My heart began to race a little at the thought of spending the entire bus ride with Ben by my side. I couldn't think of anything better.

Both the cheer and football coaches took roll and double-checked that everyone that was supposed to be aboard was present.

When our names got called, Ben and I got a couple of surprised looks and even a loud "whoop" from one of the guys.

Hoping I wasn't blushing, I stared at my legs.

Finally, the coaches were satisfied that they had everyone.

The bus rumbled to life, and we were off.

After a minute, Ben scooted toward me just a tad. "So how'd you do on that science test today?" he asked.

I sighed. "Well, let's see. I managed to not fall asleep because I only slept like five hours, but I think I got a B, at least."

He chuckled.

"What about you?" I asked him.

He seemed unsure for a minute. "Um, also a B, I hope?" He glanced at Mrs. Collins, who, by the looks of it, was already grading the tests in the front row. "I keep reminding myself to bring Mrs. Collins an apple or something."

I giggled. "Chocolate has to be the way to go. Or maybe just cold, hard cash…" I thought out loud.

Ben shook his head. "No, cash is more Mr. Chavez's style. Have you seen his car?"

We talked like that for a few more minutes.

Then he pulled out his pre-game playlist, offering me an earbud.

I took it.

By the time we got to the game, I was pumped up.

The boys played an amazing and nail-biting game, winning by just three points.

Somehow, the entire cheer squad managed not to freeze in the biting cold and icy breeze.

As we headed back to the bus, I walked close to Rachel to stay warm. We had our hoodies on, but that was it. I pointed to our skirts. "Um, yeah, we need actual pants for this kind of weather. Please pass along this suggestion to Lily and Mrs. Collins."

She grinned. "Warm-up outfits is as good as it gets, and Lily hates cheering in those." She pulled at her hoodie. "This is all you'll get during cold games, girl."

If there was one thing I missed about dance it was not having to do it in the freezing cold.

Needless to say, though, the entire bus was pumped up on the way back home because of our victory.

Apparently, this team had beat Jefferson several years in a row, and we'd finally wiped the floor with them on their turf.

As we rode home, the football coach tried to get everyone back in line, but he gave up after a while.

Someone had brought along a Bluetooth speaker so everyone was singing and pumping their fists in the air to everything from Bruno Mars to Beyonce as we traveled down a secluded highway.

One of the guys sitting behind us shook his head. "We are a horror movie waiting to happen. Bunch of cocky teens on their way home and on a road like this."

Several people laughed at that.

After a while, we stopped to eat at a Zaxby's.

I'd never been. "We don't have these where I'm from," I said, looking at the menu. "What should I get?"

Ben, Aaron, and Rachel just stared. Rachel took my hands. "Tell me you're kidding."

I shook my head. "What? Is it that good?"

Aaron shook his head but in utter disappointment. "Just order the wings and things, okay? You can thank me later."

Ben smiled. "You'll love it."

I did love it. "Oh my gosh," I said, biting another hot wing. "I'm telling my mom that we have to move here permanently. Between Bobby's and this place…I see no reason to leave."

Rachel grinned and dug into her salad. "Sounds like a done deal."

Aaron and some of his friends laughed about one of the guys on the other team who had been trash talking the entire time. Rachel began telling me about some of the moves the other cheerleaders had pulled off that she liked. Meanwhile, Ben excused himself from the table. I saw him head to the bathroom. So I focused on the delicious food in front of me.

Once everyone was done eating, we got back on the bus. Now that we were fed and full, most people put in earbuds and closed their eyes or talked quietly.

Rachel was right behind me. Because we'd gone to the bathroom just before leaving the restaurant, we were one of the last ones on the bus.

I looked for Ben and the seat we'd been in before but didn't see him. It was empty.

From one of the last rows, Aaron gave us a small wave. That was Ben next to him, but he was seated with his head leaning all the way forward and resting against the seat in front of him. I recognized the hoodie pulled over his head.

Aaron shrugged his shoulders and gave us a look like, "Sorry."

I glanced back at Rachel, who shrugged. "I guess he's tired," I said, sliding into the seat I'd been in before. Rachel joined me.

Then I remembered. He'd mentioned having to be up for an early shift at Bobby's the next day. That had to be it.

Between working every day, keeping up with homework, and all of these football games, he had to be exhausted. Especially after a tough game and a big meal.

Everything would be better the next day, I told myself. Or the next time I saw him.

But a part of me couldn't help but think that no wonder Ben had this no dating rule. Even if he liked me and wanted a girlfriend, did he have time for one? Could this even work?

25

THINGS WITH BEN didn't get better.

In fact, they only got weird.

His texts came less and less often over the next few days.

There was a good morning here and a good night there, but lots of one and two-word responses in between.

He had to be too busy to talk, right?

But when we walked to class, he hardly made eye contact, hardly talked. Something about him just seemed…off.

Before he could run off to his class, I took his hand, making him stop for a second. "Hey, are you okay? Did I do or say something?" I asked, no longer willing to debate the entire thing in my own head. It was driving me crazy.

I wanted the normal Ben back, but lately, he was acting more and more withdrawn.

Then it hit me.

Right there, while he stood and opened his mouth to say something but then closed it again.

This *was* the normal Ben. This was the exact same Ben from several weeks ago when I'd moved here. Quiet, withdrawn, hardly talked to anybody.

His hand slipped out of mine. "I'm fine. I gotta go. Talk to you later, okay?" And just like that, he was off.

I blinked back tears while I watched his retreating figure walk down the hallway.

Somehow, I had misinterpreted this whole thing.

I walked into class and took a seat, hardly paying attention to where I was going.

But he'd kissed me.

We'd talked every day.

I didn't get it.

At lunch, I told Rachel, Audrey, and Nora about it.

I stared down at my lunch, still trying to understand what had gone wrong.

Nora took my hand. "You did nothing wrong, okay? I think Ben…"

I searched her face, wondering what she was trying to say, but she didn't finish her sentence.

Rachel gave me a hug. "Ben's just…Ben. He's always been like that. It's like he's afraid to like somebody. I have no idea why."

Audrey gave me a small smile from across the table. "For the record, I think he really does like you. But something must be holding him back."

"I don't get it," Rachel said. "He's the only one who's like that." She paused. "Well, never mind. Drake is also pretty closed off too. But he'll date. He just prefers to break hearts instead of avoiding girls altogether."

Audrey turned to her. "And what about Aaron?" I could hear the teasing in her tone. "Why hasn't he asked you out yet? The winter dance is coming up, you know."

Jefferson had already seen its first couple of slightly cheesy, kinda romantic promposals.

A wide smile grew on Nora's face. "You know, I've been wondering that myself."

I wasn't sure Rachel was even capable of blushing, but she sure did stutter when she was embarrassed. "I—he, I mean, we… are just friends," she finished lamely, going back to her salad. "I don't know what you're talking about," she added under her breath.

At least that exchange made me smile. I nudged her gently. "She has a point. If you two like each other, why haven't you two…you know…"

"We don't," she said firmly. "We. Are. Just friends."

But later, Audrey pulled me aside and gave me the real reason why those two couldn't happen. "That sucks," I replied.

Cade walked by, giving Audrey a quick smile and wave.

Was it me or…

Audrey waved back. She must have noticed the way I was looking at her because she said, "We're neighbors. I live next door."

I had a feeling that there was a lot going on in and around Jefferson that I didn't know about.

Including with Ben.

Something was going on with him, and I wanted to know what.

One thing I knew for sure.

What had happened between us had been genuine. I hadn't misinterpreted anything.

But something had changed with Ben.

I wanted to know what.

26

THAT NIGHT, I turned to ice cream and rom-coms to soothe my troubles.

Mom had to work late again, but I wanted to stay up and wait for her.

I missed her.

I hadn't seen her much since she'd gotten back from that trip.

More than ever, I missed our girl talks.

Talking about boys, crushes, and funny stories. Mom always had the best stories about boys from growing up.

It was hard to imagine her at my age, worrying about a boy liking her or not and what she should say to him. If she should say anything.

I needed her advice. Desperately.

Or really, just to talk and get some reassurance that everything would be okay.

That this boy might end up totally breaking my heart, but I would be okay either way.

I needed a hug.

Well after dinner, the front door opened.

I'd been starting to snooze during The Office, just watching Jim and Pam and all the ways they couldn't be together yet but were meant for each other.

Mom walked into the living room and set down her bag and purse on the couch adjacent to me. "Hey, you. You're still up?" she asked. She sat down next to me and put her arm around me.

"Yeah," I replied, squeezing her back.

Then she eyed the empty Ben & Jerry's pint on the coffee table. "Tough day?"

I nodded, pulling back. "Boy trouble."

"Ugh," she replied. "Let me change into my pajamas, grab the other pint of ice cream, and I'll join you."

A few minutes later, though, she still wasn't back.

I began picking up my mess. Threw away the empty ice cream container.

Then I made my way to Mom's bedroom to see what was going on. Had she fallen asleep or something?

I found her sitting on her bed, laptop balanced on her legs as she typed away. "Mom?" I asked, slightly annoyed.

She hardly looked up. "Sorry, honey. I just need to reply to one email, and then we can catch up."

Something about her distracted response triggered something in me.

Why did she always have to work?

First she had to do this and then she could spend time with me, listen to me?

"Just forget about it," I snapped. "I want to go to

sleep anyway." I turned to go but Mom called out to me.

"Scarlett! I'm sorry." I faced her again. She closed the computer and patted a spot on the bed beside her. "Sit. Let's talk about it."

The problem was I no longer wanted to talk to her about anything. "I don't want to, okay? Besides, don't you have work to do? Calls to make?"

Mom's face fell as soon as the words came out of my mouth. Hurt filled her eyes along with tears. Her bottom lip quivered for just a second before she pressed her mouth into a hard line. "Okay," she replied quietly.

I bit the inside of my lip. Regret filled my insides, but I left anyway, shutting the door closed behind me.

27

ON FRIDAY, the boys lost their second game of the season.

Mom texted me at halftime that she wasn't going to make it thanks to being stuck in some serious traffic.

I sighed and let her know that it was okay, that there were still a couple of games left in the season.

Then I put away my phone. Even though I still felt bad about snapping at her, I wasn't ready to apologize just yet.

Meanwhile, during the game, Ben had missed an easy pass, costing them much needed points. It wasn't long before the rest of the team was making costly errors like that.

Coach brought Ben out for the rest of the game. It was hard to believe that one of the team's star players had gotten benched.

He slumped over with his forearms resting on his knees.

I wished I could've gone over there and reassured him, let him know that it was okay to have an off night.

On our way home, he walked past me on the bus. He hardly looked at me as he took a seat a few rows down, but his expression told me that he hated having let the whole team down.

This time, no one sat with him. He sat in the middle of the seat, earbuds in, and hood up, making it clear that he didn't want to interact with anyone.

On Monday, Ben sat by himself at lunch.

He seemed tired. First, he worked on homework, but then he seemed to give up because he put his head down on the table, resting it in his arms, face down.

I missed hanging out with him at Bobby's. Doing homework together and eating endless servings of fries.

I missed being with him, passing the time until Mom came home. Talking, laughing, noticing the way his eyes crinkled a little bit when he smiled.

How he looked down when he did smile because it was almost like he didn't want the world to see it.

I sighed and made myself stop looking over at him.

Rachel gave me a side hug. Audrey and Nora gave me sympathetic looks.

"I wish he would just say what's going on," I said, pretty bummed.

Nora glanced over at Ben, who still had his head down. "What can you expect? Boys." She turned back to us. "I swear…they're more dramatic than girls sometimes."

Rachel laughed. "Especially if it's over a freakin' video game."

Audrey gave me a serious look. "So when did he start acting all weird? I'm not saying it's your fault or anything, but do you think you said something that made him think you just wanted to be friends or something?"

I thought about that. "I don't think so?" I said, trying to remember.

Rachel snapped her fingers. "Remember on the way back from that away game? He didn't sit with you on the way back?"

I furrowed a brow. "But that night he was just tired from the game."

Rachel gave a, "Hmm." She narrowed her eyes. "I don't know. From my experience, if a guy is into you, he will want to sit with you no matter what."

Nora's eyes gleamed with mischief. "Is that why Aaron always sits with you in class? And follows you around like a puppy?"

"Oh my gosh," Rachel said. "So not true."

But I could tell she was on the verge of stuttering, which was a sure sign of her being embarrassed or trying to avoid a certain topic.

"Anyway," she went on, turning to me. "Maybe something happened before that that would explain all of this. Try to think."

I exhaled. "Let's see. We sat together on the way there. We were talking about the Human A & P test… then he told me about his little brother, how he plays football too and they pulled some prank on him…then we just listened to music the rest of the time," I finished.

Audrey, Nora, and Rachel sat for a minute, thinking.

Rachel quirked a brow. "We also stopped to eat. I remember he didn't talk much, though."

I shrugged. "Yeah, because we were eating."

"No," she said. "We were all talking and eating and then he got up and left for a while."

"Bathroom," I replied.

"Yeah," she went on. "But now that I think about it he was quiet through most of the meal."

I thought he'd been tired, but had something happened?

Rachel gasped. "You said you'd never been to Zaxby's before!"

Audrey and Nora stared quizzically at her.

So did I. "What does that have to do with anything?" I asked with a laugh.

Rachel frowned. "I don't know. It sounded way smarter in my head just a second ago."

Then it hit me. "Wait. Just before he got up and left." I tried to remember what we'd said, but it felt just out of my reach. "You and I were talking about something."

Rachel nodded. "You said something about… moving here permanently."

Audrey and Nora glanced at each other, furrowing their brows. Nora leaned forward. "What do you mean 'permanently'?" she asked me.

I shrugged. "It was a joke." But the more I thought about it, the more I saw how Ben could have thought it wasn't a joke. And really…

Had it been a joke?

Rachel, Nora, and Audrey waited for me to go on. I sighed. "I mean…it was supposed to be a joke."

Audrey looked like she was trying to figure something out. "So are you and your Mom not staying here?"

Nora nodded. "Yeah, are you guys moving back at some point?"

Rachel looked at me expectantly.

I stared down at my food. "Honestly?" I said.

They all nodded quickly.

"Honestly… I don't know," I replied. "When we decided to move here, we agreed that we would see how it went. Maybe we would stay, maybe we would move back, depending on…"

Rachel motioned with her hand. "Depending on?"

I took a deep breath. "How much I liked this new school, whether I wanted to graduate with the kids I grew up with or not, whether my mom liked her new job…" I exhaled. "And whether we wanted to move back to be close to family…and to my dad," I finished quietly.

The three of them just kind of sat back and didn't say anything for a while.

All around us, the cafeteria continued with laughter, loud conversations, and the occasional crash of someone dropping a tray or a utensil.

"Sorry, guys," I said. "I really didn't think it was that big of a deal, you know? We just moved here a few months ago. If we did move…it wouldn't be now. It would be…I don't know."

171

Rachel looked at me. "Over the summer? Before senior year?"

I nodded, cringing a little now at how it all sounded. "Yeah, probably."

Audrey set down her fork. "But you said you guys don't know yet? Like if you'll move back or not?"

I shook my head. "Nothing is set in stone," I replied. "That's what my Mom and I agreed on. We would evaluate at some point."

Rachel exhaled and put her chin in her hands. Her gaze flicked to Ben. "So maybe he thought you might be moving back? And that's why he's been acting all weird?"

Nora leaned her head to one side. "Makes sense, even if I think he could've just talked to you about it."

Audrey turned to her. "This is Ben we're talking about. He probably just decided that it was best to go back to his no dating rule."

Nora frowned. "Still…he could've talked to Scarlett about it. Let her know instead of just not talking to her anymore."

My eyes went to Ben, this time with a whole new perspective.

Is that what had happened?

As much as I thought I would be annoyed—and I had been—now I just felt kind of bad for him. I thought about that day after the pep rally, how vulnerable he'd been talking about his dad even for just a moment. I turned back to the girls.

Rachel crossed her arms and rested them on the

table. "Maybe it reminded him of his Dad too. Left a bad taste in his mouth."

Audrey nodded and turned to me. "Like he thought of his Dad leaving and then you leaving too."

Leaving? "What do you mean?" I asked. "His dad left? I thought he passed away."

Rachel shook her head. "No, he left them when they were little. Never sent them a card or called or anything."

All of a sudden, I felt like I might be sick, like I had just learned something incredibly personal about Ben and his family.

Something he should've told me himself.

But why hadn't he? He'd made it sound like his Dad had passed away too, like we'd had that in common.

I turned to look at Ben again, but he was gone.

28

IT WAS as if the universe was determined to rub in the fact that Ben and I were no longer even friends.

In fact, we were less than friends. Not even acquaintances.

More like two people who no longer even looked at each other.

Or at least one person who pretended the other one didn't exist.

I missed Ben. Missed talking to him. Missed his smiles and his text messages.

And as if it all wasn't bad enough, I missed Bobby's.

I hadn't had the courage to go back ever since Ben had stopped talking to me.

Rachel said it was ridiculous that now I was avoiding him too, but the only thing I thought was ridiculous was how fast we'd gone from more friends to less than.

And how long I'd gone without a burger and fries from Bobby's.

Ben and I had one class together.

We sat a couple of rows apart. Before, we'd smile at each other here and then, maybe send a text during class, make fun of something the teacher said.

But now it just made things all the more awkward.

However, since it was Language Arts, most of the class was reading, writing, or class discussions.

All I had to do was sit and face forward and remember to raise my hand to participate in the class discussion every once in a while.

But that day, the teacher had other ideas after the lesson.

"Okay, everyone. It's time to critique your rough drafts. So get them out and partner up with the same person as last time."

Oh no.

I pulled out my rough draft of the paper due next week along with everyone else, dreading what was coming next.

The teacher, Mrs. Brown, walked around and prodded us. "Let's go, everyone. Don't look so excited."

I moved along at a sloth's pace just like everyone else because last time I'd paired up with Ben.

This had been about three weeks ago, around when we'd kissed.

I remembered because I felt like I hadn't been able to stop blushing the entire time we worked together, just being that close to him.

Glancing around the room, I looked for any kind of escape. Nora was in this class, but today she'd been checked out for a dentist appointment.

Finally, I glanced at Ben. He looked just as nervous about this ordeal as I was.

Mrs. Brown stopped in front of my desk. "Scarlett, who did you partner up with last time?"

Uh....

"With Ben," I answered meekly.

She turned to Ben, who looked like he'd rather disappear off the face of the earth than get up from his desk. He bent down to shuffle through his book bag.

Mrs. Brown turned the empty desk in front of me over to face me in about two seconds flat. "Ben? Find your paper yet?" she asked, hands on her hips.

Ben looked at her like a deer in headlights for a second before holding ups stack of notebook paper. "Um, yes, ma'am," he replied lamely.

A minute later, we sat across from each other awkwardly without saying a word.

The rest of the class wasn't very enthusiastic about critiquing essays either, but me and Ben?

This was just painful.

I offered him my paper. "Want to read each other's paper and add comments in the margins?"

"Sure," he said, giving me his paper and taking mine.

Our fingers brushed for a second, and my breath hitched silently—I hoped.

We went back to an awkward silence, but at least this time, we had something to do.

I made my brain focus on the words in front of me and not how close Ben was. If I moved just a little, my leg would touch his, but I didn't want to do that, so I kept my legs locked in place.

This didn't need to be any worse than it already was.

After about fifteen minutes, we exchanged papers again. Ben glanced over the first page, then the second and the third. His eyes met mine, and for a second, the Ben I'd come to know was there.

But then he was back to all business. "This is great. Thank you. My comments probably aren't as helpful…"

I read over them. "No, they're good," I said, pointing to something he'd circled on the second page. "I keep forgetting to put the parenthetical citations in the right place. Thanks," I said, my voice fading into nothing.

Everyone else was still critiquing, or in some cases, completely goofing off.

I sat there, pretending to read over Ben's comments and trying to decide if Mrs. Brown would let me go to the bathroom. Maybe by the time I got back, she'd have us back at our assigned seats and we wouldn't have to do this anymore.

Just as I opened my mouth to tell Ben that I'd be right back, he said something first. "Sorry about…everything."

I stared at him. "What do you mean?" I knew what he was talking about, but I also wanted him to be more specific, to see if he would tell me what had been going on with him.

And maybe hoping that this awkward encounter had helped fix things.

Whatever there was to fix.

If at first he'd met my eyes, now he kept his gaze on his desk. "Just sorry."

I waited for him to explain why he'd gotten all weird and stopped talking to me. Because what we had before? I wanted that.

So bad.

But that's not what happened next.

He exhaled. "For leading you on. It was wrong of me."

What?

Had I heard him right?

I tried to say something, but I sat there, frozen.

Was this really happening right now?

His eyes met mine. "Why didn't you tell me?" he asked, looking utterly crushed. "Why didn't you tell me you moving here was only temporary?"

My mouth fell open, but I quickly recovered. "Because I don't know yet what we're going to do," I said, "but what I did know is that we would at least stay through the school year."

He looked down for a second.

"What did you think?" I asked, doing my best to keep my voice down. "That I would just pick up and leave from one day to the next without telling you? Is that the kind of person you think I am?"

He met my eyes for a second. "The truth is I hardly know you."

The way he said it felt like a blow to the center of my chest. "Yeah," I said, tears welling up in my eyes. "I kinda got that."

His brow furrowed. "What's that supposed to mean?"

I shrugged. "You could've told me the truth about your dad instead of letting me assume he'd died," I replied.

He leaned in, his voice became low. "What? Did you think I wanted to tell you about the worst part of my life? Do you think that's easy? That's already what defines me and my family in this town? 'They're goes poor Ben and his brothers. His mom barely makes ends meet. If only their good-for-nothing dad had stuck around,'" he mocked. "You were the one person who didn't see me that way," he added, his voice low.

I sat there, saying nothing. Worried that I was seeing him just the way he didn't want me to.

The truth was I would've given anything to wrap my arms around him and pull him close. Never let go.

But it felt like something stood between us now, something that kept me from touching Ben when I needed to.

Ben sighed. "Besides, what was the point of anything if you were just going to leave anyway?" he asked, letting his hands fall at his sides. "Huh?"

I bit the inside of my lip. "Ben, I have no idea if I'll be here next year. But I do know you're important to me, okay?" I tried.

He shook his head and turned away. "Like I said, I'm sorry. This is all my fault," he said, looking anywhere but at me. "I shouldn't have let things get this far, Scarlett. And that's on me."

With that, he got up and went back to his desk.

My neck turned hot, and tears filled my eyes, and they felt searing hot too.

Never had I fought to keep tears back harder than in that moment. Crying would be the cherry on top of this humiliation sundae.

Before I could excuse myself—more like run away —Mrs. Brown told us time was up and to head back to our seats.

I made sure Ben couldn't see my face and did my best to keep it together.

A couple of minutes later, the end of class bell went off, jerking me out of the state of shock I'd gone into.

I grabbed my bag and made for the door, not looking back and not letting the tears fall until I'd reached the bathroom.

There was no mistake now.

Ben and I were over.

29

FOR THE FIRST time that season, I skipped cheer practice and headed straight home.

I texted Lilly, letting her know that I wasn't feeling well at all.

Technically, being physically sick was the only reason we could miss practice and I didn't usually skip out on commitments lightly, but I just couldn't.

In truth, I was completely heartbroken over a boy who'd never even really been my boyfriend.

How pathetic.

As soon as I got home, I buried myself under the covers and let all the tears come.

The game-winning ball he'd given to me a while back still sat on my shelf. Looking at it and remembering Ben's sweet gesture that night stung.

In a flash, I was up. I grabbed the ball, stuffed it in the back of my closet, and shut the door before crawling back into bed.

I was angry at Ben, but mostly, I was angry at myself for falling for him.

Falling for him knowing that he didn't date or have girlfriends.

How else did I expect this to turn out?

Did I really think I was that special, that I was the one girl who would come along and make him realize that I was the exception to his rule?

I was far from special. Why would he change his rules for me?

It was evident that he wasn't going to.

I was mad at myself for falling for him from the second I'd arrived at Jefferson and locked eyes with his.

It was completely my fault I felt this way. No one else's.

I should've known better.

As I lay there and the tears slowly came to a stop, I stared up at the ceiling and thought about moving back home.

If I'd learned anything it was that sadness existed everywhere.

It existed back home in Massachusetts because of what had happened to Dad. Now it existed here because the sadness for Dad would follow us everywhere. There was nowhere we could go where it wouldn't come along with us.

And now this town also had the sadness of losing Ben.

Even thinking that felt ridiculous.

Had I ever even "had" Ben?

I was starting to think that the answer to that question was a solid no.

A couple of kisses, some texts. That's all we had been.

I thought about what he had said earlier.

He shouldn't have let things get that far.

The tears started rolling down my cheeks again in droves.

At least back in Massachusetts, there was no Ben. I'd get over him eventually.

I curled up into my blankets and let sleep take over.

It was like all the tears and sadness from the past few years had decided to come back too, and I just wanted to not think about it anymore.

At some point, the sound of my bedroom door creaking open jolted me awake.

"It's just me, honey," Mom said, walking toward me.

Luckily I'd left the lamp on my nightstand on so it wasn't completely dark.

She sat on my bed, concern etched on her face. "Are you okay? Did something happen? Are you sick?" she asked, feeling my forehead. I hadn't seen her this worried in a long time.

"I'm okay," I said, turning towards her but not meeting her eyes.

Just boys being stupid, I wanted to say.

I hated even thinking that, though, because at the end of the day, it had been my own expectations that had caused all the pain I was now in.

Never had I fallen for a boy like I had with Ben.

The one boy who had decided against dating and all that came with it.

It felt like someone had come along and punched me in the gut. It hurt so much, but instead of getting back up, I just wanted to stay on the ground and continue feeling the pain because getting up felt impossible.

No, I just wanted to stay in this bed and not see anybody, not talk to anybody.

I couldn't take one more fall.

Mom gave me a kiss on the forehead and left. I fell asleep.

Several hours later, I pulled off the covers and sat up. It was almost one in the morning. The hall light was on, and I wondered if Mom was still up.

I walked quietly toward her room, noticing that the door was open and her lamp was on. She lay kinda crooked on her bed.

It looked like Mom had literally lay down for a minute and then fallen asleep immediately.

Her phone was still in her hand and she had her work clothes on.

I couldn't help but smile at the sight of her.

But then I felt bad because I realized Mom was still mourning in a way.

Except that instead of crying in bed all day and refusing to eat, she had turned to overworking herself.

I could see it now.

Had moving here actually helped us?

It had helped me. A lot.

But maybe it had done the opposite of help Mom. I had no idea.

I didn't want to keep thinking about it, though.

Instead, I pushed Mom over a little on the bed. Then I grabbed an extra comforter from the hall closet and covered her with it.

As I left, I went to turn off her bedroom lamp, but something made me stop. On her nightstand sat an album.

I recognized it right away, but I hadn't seen it in a while. I took it back to my room and thumbed through the pages slowly.

My brain ached to go back to sleep, but I didn't want to yet.

I took my time looking at each of the pictures. This one had baby pictures of me. Mom and Dad looked so young. So happy.

In the back, there were also a few pages of them before they had me.

They'd gone on road trips and taken all kinds of random pictures.

I brushed my finger over this one picture where Dad was hugging mom so tight, and she was in the middle of laughing out loud.

Would I ever see her laugh like that again?

My mind went to the guy she'd pushed away recently. Why hadn't she just given him a chance, seen where things went?

Just like that, I thought about Ben, and the way he had pushed me away too.

The tears in my eyes appeared so fast that one hit

the picture before I could wipe it away. I soaked it up carefully with my t-shirt.

Love could be a scary thing, but it didn't have to be. That's what Mom and Ben didn't get.

I took the picture in my hands, stared at it some more, and put the album away. Then I went back to my room and got under the covers, holding that photo to my chest.

Finally, I let my eyes close, my heart beginning to break in more ways than one.

30

BEN HAD TEXTED me four words while I'd been asleep.

Ben: I really am sorry.

I didn't bother responding, not even with an *it's okay.*

The truth was I wasn't okay.

No amount of ice cream or my favorite rom-coms could fix this.

Not yet.

But I didn't want him to know that. I just wanted to numb out and not think about it anymore.

Even though I'd overslept, I felt terrible inside.

I was about to make the executive decision to skip school altogether, tell Mom that I wasn't feeling well.

But then I remembered that we had a game that afternoon. We didn't usually have games on Wednesdays, but that day we did.

I knew what I had to do.

Pick myself back up.

With a loud groan, I rolled out of bed and shuffled around my room, throwing clothes this way and that as I searched for my cheer uniform.

I finally found it under a big pile of dirty laundry.

Oops.

Mom and I scrambled out the door. Things were still a little weird. We hardly talked on the way to school. Instead, I focused on doing my best not to think about Ben. When she ordered her usual large coffee, I asked for one too.

After a late drop-off, I raced to first period.

Just as I rounded the corner, though, I bumped into someone. I stumbled back, a little coffee splashing from my Starbucks cup onto my cheer top.

"Oh, great," I mumbled.

That's what I got for walking that fast while half asleep.

I immediately dabbed at it with the napkin that had been around my cup.

This was just super.

"I feel like all I say to you these days is apologies," I heard and I finally looked up.

It was Ben.

I stopped dabbing at the coffee stain on my uniform and froze.

How was it possible for Ben to look just as tired and sleep deprived as me but still totally handsome? It just didn't make logical sense to me.

None at all.

I took a couple of steps back, almost on reflex,

because we'd been standing kinda close. "It's okay," I mumbled. "It wasn't your fault."

All of a sudden, it felt like we were talking about so much more than just bumping into each other a minute ago.

I struggled to make eye contact. "I should get to class," I said. "Sorry for running into you."

I went to walk around him, but the touch of his hand on my arm stopped me.

"Scarlett," he said. "Wait."

Just like that, his touch was gone again.

Slowly, I turned to face him again. We stood there for a second, with swarms of people moving past us on either side, but Ben didn't say anything else.

Just seeing him, being this close to him, was tough.

"I need to go," I said, walking off, not making eye contact again.

By the time the football game rolled around, I was exhausted, coffee or no coffee.

I wasn't even sure I'd head to Bobby's afterward along with everyone else. After the halftime show, I pulled my phone out of my gym bag and sent Mom a quick text, asking if she could please pick me up after the game instead of at Bobby's later.

Mom: Will do. Almost done.

We beat the other team by two touchdowns, so after the game was over, everyone was in a great mood. I hung back, letting Rachel know I was getting ready to leave.

She gave me the biggest pout but gave me a big hug goodbye.

As I made my way toward the parking lot, gym bag on my shoulder, I tried to get my mind off of Ben and everything else that had gone wrong.

Dad had left us way too soon.

Mom was still hurting.

And boys…

I wasn't sure I'd ever understand boys.

31

I WAS up before the sun the next morning.

Around five in the morning, a bad dream woke me up, and I found it impossible to sleep after that.

So I pulled on a hoodie and walked toward the window.

The sky hadn't even begun to brighten yet.

Something made me put on some sneakers and head out into the back yard.

The air was crisp and cool. It made my skin prickle. I loved it.

It reminded me of Dad and his early morning runs. I would beg to go with him sometimes, and he would always say yes, even though I always slowed him way down.

After finding a good spot, I lay down carefully on the grass, using my arms to rest my head.

The stars were still out.

I looked up at the glittering pinpoints scattered

across the night sky, immediately feeling better about everything. The last couple of days. Ben. My entire life.

There was Orion's Belt. The stars painted a familiar figure, one I'd gazed at for hours on end as a kid.

Almost as long as I could remember, I'd always looked up to find them.

It hit me then and there, laying down on the cool grass, a cool breeze sweeping over my face, why I loved the stars so much.

Those diamond-like stars had always been up there and would always be up there, at least while I remained on this Earth.

These heavenly bodies were constant. Alive and burning for millions of years.

Ironic how stars were the complete opposite of the life they shone down upon.

Friends changed. Fathers died. The remnants of those families moved.

But those stars up there?

I could always count on them to be there.

As far away as they were and wherever I ended up in this life, I knew that I could look up at the night sky and find my stars. They'd follow me everywhere.

Not everyone in my life would.

As close as people were in comparison to stars, the thing about people was that they could leave. Or end up gone forever.

But these stars would always be there.

And that's why I'd always found comfort in them.

I took a deep breath, kept my eyes locked on the constellations above me, and felt my heart lighten.

Because I knew that I would be okay.

32

I APOLOGIZED to Mom over the weekend.

It was awkward and I still felt terrible about the way I'd talked to her, but she gave me a hug anyway. Told me it was okay. "I know you didn't mean to be mean," she said.

I was proud of myself for owning up to what I'd done and saying sorry, but I could tell she still felt bad about the whole thing.

The way she still wouldn't quite meet my eyes, how she continued to mumble about making sure I had lunch money, and not quite smiling all the way…I knew I'd really hit her where it hurt.

Why had I gone and said all that stuff to her?

I wished I could take it back, but that's not the way things worked.

On Friday, we had our last home game.

Not only were things awkward at school any time I was around Ben, but things were also awkward at home with Mom.

It was like she'd sunk back into some kind of depression. She hardly ate, hardly talked. She came home and went straight to bed but still had dark circles under her eyes in the morning.

Once we pulled up to the school on Friday morning, I looked at Mom one more time. "Have a good day."

She nodded, gave me a flicker of a smile. "You too." For a moment, I thought she might say something else, but then someone honked behind us, and so I got out with one final wave.

Once I got to first period, though, I sent her a simple heart emoji.

The entire day, everyone was more pumped than usual. I wore my cheer top along with the rest of the squad. Since this was the last home football game of the season, it was a pretty big deal.

Most, if not all, of the school would be there.

Our usual halftime routine was going to be bigger and better than ever. That was the plan anyway. As the time for the game drew closer, I prayed that I wouldn't choke again like at the pep rally.

I definitely wasn't eager for another gigantic embarrassing moment in front of the entire school. So I pushed away all the crappy feelings around Mom and Ben and just pasted a big smile on.

Just before the game, the squad and I got ready in the girls' locker room, putting finishing touches on make-up and hair.

I focused on the loud and upbeat music, letting it define my mood instead of all the negative self-talk going on inside my head. That could wait until tomorrow. Tonight, I needed to go out there and do my best. The squad was counting on me.

As I exhaled, I couldn't help but think about Ben, what he had to be thinking in that moment.

Was he also pumping himself up? Pushing away all the nervous thoughts? Maybe he was looking at himself in the mirror like me and telling himself that he had a game to win.

Not because football was so important but because it was one small step toward a better life for him and his family. Towards proving himself.

If I'd learned anything about Ben, it had to be that.

His drive, his unwillingness to give up.

I blinked back at myself in the mirror.

It's why he'd said no to me in the end.

No room for unimportant things like love.

I wasn't a part of his plan.

How could I ever be mad at him for that?

I took a deep breath.

Slowly, I was making peace over what had happened with us.

He led the team through the large paper banner that read GO ELEPHANTS! WIN, WIN, WIN. The crowd went wild, and so did the cheerleaders.

Rachel did several back flips, landing the last one perfectly. The people in the stands went even crazier.

As the game began and the first play was executed, the cheer squads from both schools cheered back and forth.

We clapped, we stomped, we chanted like victory depended on it. And in a way, it did.

By halftime, we were down three points, which meant the game could still go either way.

If the boys won tonight, they'd have a spot at state. If not, this was their last game of the season, so there was a lot riding on how they did.

Ben had already missed one pass, and like the crowd, I could tell something was off with him. He didn't miss easy passes, and I could tell from the frustration on his face that he wasn't happy about it.

For about half a second, I thought about going up to him, reminding him that he'd completed how many passes in his life already? There was nothing that he couldn't do.

I bit my lip. No, I was the last person he would want to see.

He came off the field for half-time, and our eyes met.

I shot him a quick thumbs up, hoping it communicated that I was rooting for him, no matter what.

For a second, I thought he might smile, but then he turned and jogged toward the boys' locker room along with the rest of the football team.

Lilly called us to get ready, and I remembered that I was supposed to be paying attention. I had to get in place.

We ran to the middle of the football field, pom-poms in hand.

After I found my spot beside Rachel, I turned to face the crowd.

Rachel's voice could barely be heard above the chaos that was the stands. "Let's kill it, girls!" she yelled.

This was it. Our big moment as a squad.

Go big or go home, right?

Despite everything that had happened, all the sadness in my life, I was going to go big.

Most of the crowd had gone quiet in anticipation of the show, but a scream erupted from somewhere high up.

The voice sounded kind of familiar…

There. Two waving pom-poms grabbed my attention.

I squinted my eyes. And was that a red and gold uniform just like ours?

Another scream. I recognized the dark hair. "Go elephants!"

Oh. My. Gosh.

Rachel looked at me for a second. "Scarlett, is that your mom?"

I smiled wide, not believing my own eyes. "It is my mom."

Mom waved at me again, and I waved back. Then she blew me a kiss. I did the same, going from disbelief to laughter.

Lilly called over to me. "Um, are we putting on a show or… are we putting on a show?" she asked sarcastically.

I grinned at her and then Rachel. Whatever pain I still felt, it could wait until after tonight. "Let's do this."

33

AS SOON AS the game resumed, the opposing team scored a scathing touchdown.

The coach looked furious, and it only got worse when Ben dropped an easy pass right after that.

The squad had executed an excellent half-time routine, but the boys? They were struggling, big time.

This was an important game, and if they kept this up, they were done for the season.

Rachel grimaced as the coach called for a timeout and then signaled for Ben to come off the field. "If they don't go to state this year, that'll be the first time in like a decade or something."

I grimaced too, my gaze on Ben. He looked dejected, hanging his head as the Coach chewed him out for dropping such an easy pass.

The crowd had quieted down just watching the scene unfold, and I felt embarrassed for Ben. We were close enough to the bench to decipher Coach's angry words. "The Ben that played the first game...I need him here tonight. He's not. I don't know what's going on with you, Garcia, but you've got two choices. Either get it together, or do your team a favor and step off my field, son."

The words stung for me too. I couldn't imagine how Ben felt.

Humiliated. Frustrated. Like giving up, probably.

With his helmet still in his hands, Ben stood there for a second. Everyone waited with bated breath, wondering if he really was thinking of getting off the field.

Without even thinking about it, I took a step toward him.

He had to keep playing. The team was counting on him.

So what if he had messed up a couple of plays? They still had time to win. A few errors didn't erase all of his hard work and talent.

I wanted to scream that at him, but I also knew this wasn't up to me, wasn't my decision.

The seconds ticked on by, and I, along with everyone else, waited for Ben to turn around and get back on the field, especially when the referee blew the whistle.

It was now or never.

Come on, Ben, I pleaded silently. You can do this.

But he didn't step back onto the field.

He stepped off.

Without a second look to the coach, Ben jogged off.

For a second, I wondered if he was heading to the locker room, but he wasn't. He was heading in the opposite direction, toward the table sitting along the first line of the stands.

Several people sat at that table, including the people who kept score and the guy who spoke into the mic whenever something important happened, like an interception or a touchdown or something.

He spoke into the mic once he realized what was going on. "What is Benjamin Garcia doing?" he began. "Oh, maybe he'd like to take over my job," he added with a chuckle.

Ben went right up to him, said something to him.

I glanced around at the rest of the girls. Lilly, Rachel, and everyone else seemed just as engrossed in what was happening as the people in the stands.

We normally didn't just stand there and not cheer, but that was exactly what was happening.

The entire stadium had gone pretty quiet, except for whispers and mumblings, of course.

Ben turned so he was kind of facing the crowd and kind of facing the field.

The entire game had stopped. All attention was on him.

Coach looked entirely dumbfounded, like he couldn't comprehend any reason why one of his star players had decided to do this.

Whatever "this" was.

Slowly, Ben pulled the mic up to his mouth.

His eyes slid from the crowd to the student band to us.

Then his gaze met mine.

I froze.

"Oh. My. Gosh," I heard Rachel whisper.

Uh, same.

Why was Ben looking at me like that?

More than ever, I wished I knew magic because all I wanted to do was disappear.

Ben spoke into the mic. "I'm sorry, everyone. I just had to...well, see, I've been playing like crap tonight because something's not right, and I need to make it right."

Was this really happening?

He went on. "You see, this amazing and beautiful girl stepped into my life recently, and instead of seeing that, I ran away scared. Scared that...like other important people in my life...she would leave. But I was wrong. I don't want to live my life in fear of what might happen. That's no life at all," he said.

A few people began clapping at his words.

But he wasn't done yet. "Scarlett," Ben said, his voice booming loud. "I'm sorry for being a jerk. And if you'll still have me, I'd love it if you would be my date to the winter dance."

He brought the mic back down, set it down on the table beside him, but his eyes remained locked on mine.

All of a sudden, it felt like everyone's eyes were on me.

I fought the urge to run because I realized that Ben —and every single person in the stands—was waiting for an answer.

"Say something!" Rachel whisper shouted behind a wide smile.

Right.

I opened my mouth to speak. "Yes," I said.

But I could tell from Ben's face that he wasn't sure what I'd said. So I nodded several times. "Yes!"

Rachel began screaming and waving her pom-poms. Only a second later, the rest of the squad followed suit.

Lilly called out a cheer called YES and I wondered what I was supposed to do. Follow along? Stand there awkwardly?

Then Rachel, being Rachel, ran several feet along the side of the football field before launching herself into the air, pulling off about five backflips.

That's when the crowd began to go wild.

I turned to Rachel and then Ben.

Rachel urged me toward Ben.

Ben began walking toward me, a huge smile on his face.

Slowly, I relaxed and began matching my smile to his. Complete with full-on cheddar and everything as I walked.

The closer we got, the faster we moved until I landed in his arms.

Even feeling Ben against me, I couldn't believe this was real, that this was actually happening.

How had my life turned into a freakin' Netflix movie??

Ben looked down at me, still grinning. "Can we try this again?" he asked quietly.

I nodded. "I'd love that."

Then he kissed me, and I legit wondered if I was in the middle of a crazy dream.

The announcer guy's voice brought us back down to

Earth. "I should've known that girl troubles were behind this player's game being off tonight," he said with a chuckle.

Some of the people in the stand began to laugh too. Others began to clap and cheer.

Ben laughed too, and I couldn't help but join him. "You really know how to grab a girl's attention," I quipped.

"I do, huh?" he replied. The sound of the ref's whistle ended the moment. He glanced back to the field. "I…should get going, though."

I nodded. "You probably should."

He kissed me on the forehead then said, "See you after the game, Scarlett."

34

BEN WALKED off the football field and toward me, a large golden trophy in his hand.

I took him in, football uniform and all, not believing how handsome my boyfriend was.

"You did it," I cried, dropping my pom-poms so I could hug him.

He grinned and held up the trophy. "Not too shabby, huh?"

"Not shabby at all," I replied, giving him a hug.

Aaron and a couple of other guys came up to us, patting Ben on the back.

He handed them the trophy and turned back to me, pulling me aside. "Now that the football season is over, not to mention cheer, I'm gonna have more time for us," he said.

I gave his hand a squeeze. "That sounds good to me. And speaking of the football season being over…"

I walked over to where my gym bag lay in the grass

and pulled out a bag of cookies. "For you," I said, handing him the bag.

Ben smiled as our eyes met. "I still remember the day you tackled me to the ground after you found out about my peanut allergy," he said, amused.

I laughed and looked down. "Me too."

He pulled me in close. "I think that's the day I realized how much I liked you," he said quietly.

I wrapped my arms around his neck, finding it hard to focus on breathing. Just like that, I was back to not being able to form sentences. "Really?" I breathed. After a second, I worked up the courage to tell him what was on my mind. "For me, it was the moment we bumped into each other my first day."

He chuckled. "I won't lie. I thought you were a little weird. Cute but weird."

I laughed, even if part of me wanted to die from mortification. I knew it!

Mom came up to us, and we pulled apart. Ben shook her hand. "Hey, Mrs. Moore."

"Ben," she replied with a smile. "Great game."

"Thank you," he said. "Couldn't have done it without your screams of encouragement from the stands."

Now Mom looked a little embarrassed. She brought her hand to her chest. "Oh, you could hear me all the way on the field?"

I grinned wide at her.

"Yes, ma'am," Ben replied. I could tell he was trying not to laugh.

Mom cleared her throat. "Well, I'm glad it helped."

The football coach called Ben over, and he gave me a peck on the cheek before running off.

Mom and I stared after him. "I like him," she said. "I'm glad things ended up working out between you two."

I sighed. "Me too."

She turned back to me. "So I'm going out with that guy from work next week," she said.

"Really?" I asked, surprised. "What made you change your mind?"

She shrugged. "I just figure if you're brave enough to start over at a new school and open up your heart to the possibility of love, then maybe I want to be brave too."

I wrapped her in a hug. "I'm glad we moved here."

She hugged me back. "Me too. I think we needed this more than we knew. I love this town, as much as I miss our old home."

It definitely felt like home.

She tucked some hair behind my ear. "I know we said we would give it time before we made a final decision on staying here, but I want you to know that it's your decision, okay?"

"We said we would make it together," I replied, nervous all of a sudden. It was a big decision, and the thought of making it alone was scary.

She smiled. "Yeah, but it's your senior year next year. I'll be fine no matter where I am. We're together, and that's all that matters to me. If you decide you want to move back and graduate with your old friends or if you just want to be closer to Dad, I'm okay with that.

And if you decide that you want to stay here instead, I'm okay with that too."

I exhaled. Tried to think about it, but it wasn't the kind of thing that I wanted to rush. That I knew for sure.

Being close to Dad at graduation, being able to go see him afterward and even feeling like he was close would mean a lot.

But Ben, Rachel, Audrey, and Nora meant a lot too.

"Okay," I said. "I'll think about it."

Mom brushed my face with her thumb. "There's no wrong decision, okay? Either way, we'll be fine, and you have plenty of time to decide."

Mom's phone rang, and she glanced at it. "I'll see you at home, okay?"

We hugged goodbye, and she walked off, talking on the phone.

I looked off toward Ben who was still talking to his coach and a couple of older men. It looked like a serious conversation, and I wondered if those were scouts he was talking to.

Maybe Ben had some big decisions of his own to make.

It all made me nervous, but one thing I knew for sure.

We would be okay. Things had a way of working out.

35

LIGHT REFLECTED off the silver snowflake decorations hanging from the ceiling.

I pulled Ben closer as we swayed to the slow music playing in the background.

He squeezed my hand and then twirled me around. My sparkly silver dress caught the light too. It was a strapless sweetheart neckline design. It hugged my figure all the way down to my knees before flaring out.

As soon as Mom had seen it at the mall, she'd pointed it out. "That one," she'd blurted out.

I'd immediately shaken my head. No way could I pull that kind of dress off. "I should go for something safer," I'd replied.

Mom had looked at me and scoffed. "Safe? Please… this dress was made for you. Just watch." And she'd walked right over and grabbed it before hauling me off to the dressing room to try it on.

She'd been right.

The dress fit me perfectly.

And playing it safe? Not something I planned to do in the future.

Because the thing about life was that we weren't guaranteed anything.

Tragedy happened. Losses occurred.

So why play it safe?

Why not go after exactly what you want?

Mom and I had taken the risk of moving out here. She'd taken that new job.

I'd wanted to play it safe, though, from the moment I got here.

But somehow I'd learned to take risks and start living again.

First it was cheer.

Then it was falling for Ben.

Getting hurt in the process.

But even if I wasn't dancing with him in the middle of the dance floor right now, I still wouldn't change a thing.

With everything that had happened to me already, because of my Dad passing away out of nowhere...I wanted to make sure that I didn't live life on the sidelines.

Dad had truly lived life every single day. Going after his dreams, living life to the fullest and bringing us along for the ride.

I knew that he would want me to do the same.

I still had no idea if I'd be at Jefferson High my senior year. I told Mom that I'd let her know for sure by the summer.

But I had a feeling we might end up staying.

I had made friends. I had Ben, and I was happier than I'd been in a long time, even if I missed visiting Dad.

Mom's schedule was tough, but she was learning to manage it all. Besides, she had a feeling she might get that promotion she'd been hoping for.

It would mean more money and more time together. Time to maybe travel and explore the world.

Dad had always wanted to do that, and we wanted to do it for him since he was gone.

So as much as I really liked Ben, I knew there was a good chance of me leaving sooner or later.

But that was true for both of us anyway.

High school wasn't forever.

College was around the corner. He had big dreams too.

But we'd talked about it, and we were determined to take this amazing thing called life one day at a time and no more.

Besides, that was all we could really count on, right?

I'd made my peace with that.

No more playing it safe. No more waiting for tomorrow.

The song ended and an upbeat song began playing.

Ben came in close. "Want something to drink?" he asked loudly.

I nodded. "That would be great."

As he walked off in search of the punch bowl, I looked for Rachel.

There she was. Standing on the sidelines. Arms crossed, looking not so happy despite looking like a freakin' model in her sequined navy blue dress and long romantic waves.

I had to find out why. "Why aren't you out there dancing?" I demanded.

She opened her mouth to say something but then deflated like a balloon. "It's…complicated."

I shrugged. "Why does it have to be complicated?" I asked. "Make it uncomplicated."

She glanced away. Aaron was over there, looking just as not happy as Rachel.

We were going to have to do something about this. That I knew.

I walked over there.

"Scarlett!" Rachel called after me, but I kept going anyway.

I went up to Aaron, who looked just as handsome as Ben in a super nice suit. What was it in the genes of the Garcia brothers? "Hey," I told him. "Why haven't you asked Rachel to dance?"

He exhaled and shoved his hands in his pockets. "Did she tell you to come over here and ask me that? Is she mad at me?"

I eased up on him a little. "She's not mad. Promise," I said. "But it's sooo obvious you're dying to dance with her, and she with you. So why not go over there?"

Aaron's gaze went to the floor. After a minute, he looked up and said, "You know, I've never seen Ben this happy before. Ever. We have you to thank for that."

He'd caught me off guard with those words so I had no idea what to say.

"He's always put so much pressure on himself to be

the perfect son, the perfect football player, even the perfect employee. But I'm glad he's finally seeing that his own happiness comes first," Aaron went on. "That's what's really important."

Before he could say anything else, Ben came up to us, two plastic glasses full of punch in his hands. "Want to get some fresh air?" he asked. Then he gave his brother a quick wave and grin.

"Sure," I said. Before I followed him toward the garden outside, I looked back at Aaron. "This conversation isn't done."

He smiled. "Okay."

If anyone deserved to be happy, it was Rachel and Aaron. They were absolutely adorable together, and I was going to make it my mission to bring them together, no matter what.

But first, I had a very cute boy to dance with all evening.

We finished our drinks and stared up at the stars together for a few minutes.

As Ben stood behind me, his arms wrapped around me, I couldn't help but think that I never wanted to forget this moment. No matter what happened tomorrow or next year.

I just wanted to take everything in and savor it.

From Ben's sweet kisses to his perfect smile to the way his touch felt on the small of my back.

Nothing was impossible. Not the good or the bad.

And I was okay with that.

We would be okay.

36

AARON

RACHEL LOOKED STUNNING TONIGHT.

My brain battled between going up to her, taking her hand, and leading her onto the dance floor…and staying put.

I stayed put.

Ben led Scarlett outside, his hand in hers.

I'd meant what I'd said to her earlier. I'd never seen him so happy before.

Ever.

And more than anyone, he deserved it.

Always working to help Mom cover the bills, killing it on the football field, and taking care of the rest of us since we'd been kids, even though he was hardly older than the rest of us.

He'd always seemed older.

But he was just a kid who deserved to have fun and make the most of life. I was glad Scarlett was the kind of girl who would teach him just that.

The sight of one of the linebackers going up to Rachel had my attention back on her.

Was he seriously going to ask her to dance?

Anger surged through me, and for a second, I wished I was the one with the courage to ask her for a dance.

But I just couldn't.

There were times when I wished that I didn't feel the way I did about her, but it was impossible.

Rachel paused and flashed her gaze at me. I immediately looked away.

When I looked at her again, she was on the dance floor with said linebacker.

And me? I wanted to punch something.

I hated the way she had her arms on his shoulders, how his hands were on her waist.

That was supposed to be us.

But thanks to fate and friendship, it never could be.

Drake came up to me, his gaze immediately going to where mine was. He laughed a little. "I told you. You need to get over her, once and for all. Either ask her out or get rid of the puppy love."

Unlike Ben and me, Drake was in black jeans and a slightly ripped t-shirt. He purposely went against the grain, and he liked to tell things how he saw them.

He was right. I needed to get over Rachel, especially if I was too chicken to even ask her for a dance.

Drake left, and as soon as he did, I saw why.

Rachel's brother, David, came up to me. Like Drake, his gaze followed mine.

David was also my best friend. And had been since preschool.

He frowned and did a double take. "I know that's not Kenneth with my sister."

The thing about David was that, according to him, no guy within a thousand miles would ever be good enough for his sister.

And he had a point.

She'd been hurt in the past, and he was determined to protect her at all costs.

Rachel, though… she was everything you could want in a girl.

Beautiful and hot. Charming and smart. A good girl overall but sassy at times.

She drove me wild.

But she was the one girl I could never ask out.

David would never go for it. And if there was one thing that hurt more than the idea of never being with Rachel, it was losing David as a friend.

Not after everything.

So I stood on the sidelines and watched Rachel dance with someone else.

Her and me? It just wasn't in the cards.

AUTHOR'S NOTE

THIS PARTICULAR BOOK means a lot to me.

It's April 2020 as I write this. The last time I wrote and published a book was in June/July 2019.

Since then, my life has changed completely. I've gone through things I never thought I'd have to face, and it took a toll on me for a while.

For months, I couldn't write, couldn't create.

In January, I finally felt ready again. Made myself sit down and do it.

I wrote this book. And I also made it through everything life came at me with.

There have been incredibly hard moments, but I came out on the other side stronger and more determined than ever to reach my biggest goals.

More committed than ever to keep creating.

I want to take a moment to thank my readers for being patient, asking how I was doing, and supporting me and my work.

I can't tell you how much it means.

Thank you.

I'm so excited for this new series. It's an idea that I began hatching almost a year ago, and I'm incredibly happy that the first book is finally out.

But mostly, I'm ecstatic to be writing again.

I can't wait to hear what you guys think of this one.

Let me know :)

You can email me and say hi at hello@yeseniavargas.com
Thanks so much for reading…

Yesenia

P.S. A fun fact about Ben's jersey number, 28: it's age I am now. I chose that number as a symbol of everything I've gone through up until now. I don't think things should've happened any other
way. I wouldn't be who I am today if it weren't for all of it <3

P.P.S. Don't miss Aaron's story! Preorder Dating Aaron & Other Forbidden Things here: https://amzn.to/3bVjRtx

P.P.P.S. Make sure you sign up for my newsletter.

You'll get notified of **special VIP Reader pricing** when the next book in the series is out!

Sign up for my newsletter and become a VIP Reader here: https://www.yeseniavargas.com/garcia1

ACKNOWLEDGMENTS

I couldn't have written this book without the love of my daughters. Thank you. I love you guys more every day that goes by.

A big thank you to Sally for tearing this book apart for me and helping me make it the best it can be. I really appreciate it.

Another huge thank you to Jenny at Seedlings for creating this beautiful book cover.

Thank you to my friends, for listening and making me laugh.

And, of course, last but certainly not least, a huge heartfelt thank you to you. I couldn't do what I love if it weren't for awesome readers like you :)

ABOUT THE AUTHOR

Yesenia Vargas is the author of several young adult romance books. Her love for writing stories was born from her love of reading and books. She has her third grade teacher to thank for that.

In addition to writing and reading, she spends her time hanging out with her family, working out, and binge-watching Netflix. In 2013, she graduated from the University of Georgia, the first in her family to go to college.

Yesenia lives in Georgia with her two daughters. She also blogs at writermom.net.

Check out what she's up to at yeseniavargas.com.

facebook.com/YeseniaVargasWriter

instagram.com/thisiswritermom

ALSO BY YESENIA VARGAS

#BestFriendsForever Series

#TheRealCinderella

#LoveToHateThatBoy

#GoodGirlBadBoy

#TheBoyfriendDare

#AllIWantForChristmas

#BreakingTheRules

#MeantToBe

Boys of Summer

Falling for the Rich Boy

Find all the download links as well as a complete list of my
most recent books at yeseniavargas.com/books/